DIANA
and the Island of No Return

WONDER WOMAN™ ADVENTURES

DIANA and the Island of No Return

Aisha Saeed

A Yearling Book

Wonder Woman created by William Moulton Marston

Cover art by Alessia Trunfio

 Published in the United States by Yearling, an imprint of Random House Children's Books, a division of Penguin Random House LLC, New York. Originally published in hardcover in the United States by Random House Children's Books, a division of Penguin Random House LLC, New York, in 2020.

Yearling and the jumping horse design are registered trademarks of Penguin Random House LLC.

Visit us on the Web! rhcbooks.com

Educators and librarians, for a variety of teaching tools, visit us at RHTeachersLibrarians.com

The Library of Congress has cataloged the hardcover edition of this work as follows:
Names: Saeed, Aisha, author.
Title: Diana and the island of no return / Aisha Saeed.
Description: New York : Random House, [2020] | Series: Wonder Woman adventures | Audience: Ages 8–12. | Audience: Grades 4–6. |
Summary: Twelve-year-old Diana's much-anticipated visit with her best friend, Princess Sakina, turns into an adventure as they face a booby-trapped island, a forbidden visitor, and a demon.
Identifiers: LCCN 2019052960 (print) | LCCN 2019052961 (ebook) | ISBN 978-0-593-17447-0 (hardcover) | ISBN 978-0-593-17448-7 (library binding) | ISBN 978-0-593-17449-4 (ebook)
Subjects: CYAC: Adventure and adventurers—Fiction. | Best friends—Fiction. | Friendship—Fiction. | Princesses—Fiction.
Classification: LCC PZ7.1.S24 Di 2020 (print) | LCC PZ7.1.S24 (ebook) | DDC [Fic]—dc23

ISBN 978-0-593-17836-2 (paperback)

Printed in the United States of America
10 9 8 7 6 5 4 3 2
First Yearling Edition 2021

For Malala, Greta, Mari,
and all the other real-life superheroes

Chapter One

When Diana looked back upon this day, she would remember many things: the way the sun beat down upon her where she sat, perched on the highest branch of the largest olive tree jutting out from the cliffs of Themyscira. The laughter of the women beneath her setting up tents and stalls for the Chará festival. The gardeners hurriedly sweeping leaves from the pathways and trimming the last of the rosebushes surrounding her palace home. This was also the day her life would completely change forever.

Of course, at the moment, Diana had no idea of the danger that lay in wait for her a few short hours later. This particular afternoon, she craned her neck, searching the horizon for the ships that would soon arrive. Time always felt like it slowed down the more she looked forward to something, but she couldn't help feeling excited about this week. Her best friend, Sakina, was almost here. Visitors were rare on Themyscira. Her mother, Queen Hippolyta, had created their nation as a safe place, far from the world of men and all their war and strife. The women who lived on the island were here, in part, because they did not wish to be found.

The Chará festival was the one exception to this rule. In a little while, their island nation of jagged cliffs, stone temples, and sweeping seaside vistas would fill with the most esteemed women in the world: leaders, artists, welders, carpenters, and fierce warriors from distant lands. As always, there would be no men—they were strictly prohibited on Themyscira. Diana had never met one in her life.

Her mother would stay busy in meetings with world leaders for much of the week, but Diana loved exploring the tented stalls to try out the latest technology in steel plate armor or to gaze in wonder at the pottery and paintings artisans had brought with them from around the world. Last summer was the first year Sakina and Diana were allowed to take part in lessons offered by experts in their respective specialties. Sewing, welding, woodwork . . . The girls tried them all. Diana remembered the wooden dolls with the matching lopsided grins they'd carved—she still laughed any time she saw the creation resting on her bedroom shelf.

A battle cry sounded in the distance. Diana glanced at the grassy coliseum shaded by a grove of olive trees at the island's center. Columns with marble statues of the goddesses Athena, Artemis, and Hera gazed down on the Amazon warriors who, with swords drawn, were finishing the last of their martial arts lessons before the festival was to begin. A familiar wistful tug pulled at Diana's heart as she watched the women swivel and twirl with their weapons like graceful dancers in silver and bronze plate armor. More than anything in the world, she longed to train alongside them.

Just then a bird trilled near her ears.

"Mira!" Diana exclaimed. The creature was blue as the ocean, with gold-tipped wings and a ruby-red tail that fanned out like a peacock's. She belonged to Sakina. The bird served as their messenger, shuttling notes to and fro while the girls were apart.

The bird settled on Diana's lap and blinked her silvery eyes. At night they shone like beams through the dark skies; the girls had had many adventures through the island's forest last summer with Mira's eyes shining the way. Diana smiled. If the bird was here, studying the horizon with her, it meant that Sakina's ship couldn't be too far behind.

Diana looked back at the island. A flash of gold glinted in the distance. Her eyes widened. It was Cylinda and Yen, the newest warriors to arrive on the island. They wore red metallic masks and gold plate armor, which meant only one thing: they were headed to the island's edge to guard Doom's Doorway. The plain concrete barrier separated Themyscira from the sinister Underworld, ruled by the god Hades. The Amazons were tasked with the important duty of guarding it and keeping the creatures and lost souls who were meant to stay within the Underworld from escaping.

Scrambling from the tree, Diana swept down the

stone steps etched into the cliff, past the women setting up a weaponry display beneath a white tent, and over to the two warriors.

"What are you doing?" Diana demanded once she caught up to them.

"Hello to you, too," Yen replied. She tucked a strand of dark hair behind her ear. At six feet tall, both Cylinda and Yen towered over Diana. "Heading to the door. We're relieving Lisbeth and Kajol."

"But it can't be your turn already. You were there last week."

"The queen asked for volunteers," Cylinda said.

"What about the festival?"

"Everyone wants to attend." Yen shrugged. "We figured as the newest, we should be the ones to take an extra shift."

"You don't understand. The Chará festival is *incredible,*" Diana insisted. "You can't miss your first one!"

"The bazaar does seem like fun," Cylinda said. She slid her mask from her face and looked wistfully at the stalls. From where they stood, the many tables extended beyond their line of sight. In a few hours they would be filled with weaponry, artwork, and clothing from around the world.

"It's not just the bazaar," Diana said. As recent arrivals, the two women were still learning how to battle and fight. "There are classes and workshops on all sorts of things. Aunt Antiope is teaching a sword fighting masterclass this year. You know the kita hold you've been working on? She's doing a whole day of lessons on it for the visitors."

"Lucky for us, we're not visitors." Yen smiled. "We'll work on it once we're back from our duties. Sweet of you to be concerned, but there will be other Chará festivals in the years to come."

"Take notes for us?" Cylinda asked. "Especially on what the most popular weapon is these days. Yen and I have a bet going."

"The most popular?" Diana scoffed. "It's better to focus on what the *best* weapon is, and that's easy." She walked to the weaponry table and lifted a bronze sword.

"The butterfly sword? I thought you'd point out the Limina." Cylinda cocked her head to the side. "The jagged edge on that one is three times as long."

"That's the problem with it: it's *too* long. The butterfly is lighter than any other, which keeps you fast on your feet." Diana lifted the sword and flung it skyward. It twirled like an acrobat. Diana grabbed it and sliced an *X* in the air.

"Point taken." Yen raised her hands and laughed. "We don't ever want to be on your bad side."

"Diana." A familiar voice interrupted them.

Diana lowered the sword. Her smile faded. Her mother, Queen Hippolyta, approached the three of them and crossed her arms. She wore her usual golden dress paired with golden plate armor, her blond hair swept up as it always was, and a mixture of exasperation and disappointment in her bright blue eyes. This was usual, too.

"She was only showing us her favorite weapon," Yen hurriedly said. "It was completely innocent."

"It always is," her mother said.

Diana walked back to the table and set the sword down. Her mother didn't say anything more. She didn't need to. They'd had the conversation so many times, Diana had practically memorized it. And yet no explanation her mother gave ever made any sense. How could Diana live among the Amazon warriors, the fiercest fighters in the world, and not be allowed to train beyond the basics? The frustration burned inside her.

"Are you ready for duty?" her mother asked them. "You both did an excellent job last time."

"It's an honor to serve." Cylinda beamed.

"The door's stayed shut as long as I've been alive," Diana insisted. "Maybe they could leave their post for a little while today. An hour or two, just to take a peek at the festival."

"It's our responsibility to guard the passage to the Underworld," her mother said. "And as dull as it can feel sometimes, preventing a problem is less troublesome than fixing one."

"Update us on everything when we return?" Cylinda ruffled Diana's hair. Diana nodded and promised she would, and Yen winked as they left to report for duty.

Once the warriors were out of earshot, Diana swiveled to her mother.

"You didn't have to embarrass me in front of

them," she said. "I was only holding the weapon."

"And twirling it in the air. Diana, you're not supposed to handle unfamiliar weapons, especially those specialty ones on the table."

"But did you see me with it?" Diana insisted. "Both Cylinda and Yen were impressed."

"Be that as it may, you are not equipped to use it."

"Then maybe it's time to let me train," Diana countered.

"Diana." Her mother sighed. "Not this again."

"Why not? I'm twelve. Not two. It's about time I'm allowed."

"You have trained plenty. Your aunt taught you all the basics, and you even have a weapon of your own."

"This lousy sword? It won't hurt a fly." Diana gestured to the silver weapon sheathed at her waist. She'd decorated the hilt with emeralds a few days earlier, but it didn't change the fact that it was still an unremarkable sword. "Besides, I want to know more than the basics. How can I live on an island of Amazons and not be a warrior?"

"That's precisely *why* you don't need to be one," her mother said. She rested a hand on Diana's shoulder. "You don't know what some of these women have seen, the tragedies and scars that brought them to Themyscira. You were born here, safe and secure from the dangers of this world."

"But what if something happened here and—"

"If anything were to happen, we have plenty of fully trained warriors on hand to help us. Time is a gift, Diana. Use it for other things. Sharpen your mind. Focus on other things that matter."

Diana knew her mother wouldn't budge, but her stomach still twisted with disappointment. She studied the golden cuffs around her wrists, the same ones worn by all the Amazons in Themyscira.

"Even if there's no *practical* need to train," Diana said, "why isn't my *wanting* to reason enough?"

The queen studied her for a moment.

"Diana," she finally said. "I love you. You know that, don't you? I love you so much, I formed you out of clay myself. I don't enjoy keeping you from your dreams. Perhaps when you're older we will discuss this again—when you can understand more about who you are."

"Who I am?" Diana said with a start. This was new.

"I shouldn't have said anything." Her mother looked away.

"Please, Mother," Diana pleaded. "Is there some reason you haven't shared with me for why you don't want me to train?"

"The festival is about to begin," Queen Hippolyta said gently. "After the week concludes, you and I can have a long conversation and—"

"The boats!" a woman cried out.

Diana shifted her gaze. Ships were at last pulling up to the docks. Hulking vessels swaying in the ocean, waves sloshing against their sides. More of them filled the bright horizon in the distance, their sails all different colors—crimson, blue, yellow, and white—and fluttering against the wind. An adviser approached her mother and whispered in the queen's ear. Diana pushed away her disappointment. The moment was over.

***

Walking over to the wooden docks that stretched into the sea, Diana scanned the insignias of the arriving ships. She recognized many of them from years past. There was the mortar and pestle stitched on the Ruhas' sails—they were a healing community to the south. The welders of Baltin had pulled in as well, a brazing rod tinged with red etched into the side of their hull. At last, Diana found the ship she was searching for: the white sail embroidered with a golden quill and unfurled scroll. Diana smiled. It was the Scholars' ship. The Scholars were the keepers of the world's vastest libraries and proudly boasted the most competitive higher-learning institutions. Sakina was among their people.

"Well, look who it is!" a voice called out. Sakina emerged from the boat. Her dark hair was pulled back, and she wore a maroon tunic, golden leggings, and brown leather boots laced to her knees. Waving to Diana, she hurried toward her.

The girls embraced.

"I seriously thought summer would never come!"

Sakina exclaimed, pulling back. "I swear it took triple the time for this week to arrive."

"I felt the exact same way!" Diana said.

"Even an ocean apart, we're still on the same wavelength, huh?"

"No surprise there." Diana laughed.

Sakina glanced down at Diana's brown belt.

"New sword?" she asked.

"I wish," Diana said. "It's the same one as last time. I added these jewels to mix things up."

"Nice! I'm a sucker for emeralds." A mischievous look glinted in Sakina's brown eyes. "And aren't you going to say anything about *my* new sword?"

Sure enough, Sakina had a leather belt strapped around her waist, much like Diana. A golden hilt poked out from her right side.

"Really?" Diana exclaimed. "Your parents let you have a sword?"

"Yep. I'd been begging for one ever since last summer. And watch this!" Sakina pulled out her bronze sword and flicked her wrist. Out of the hilt of the sword popped a quill. "It's basically perfect, don't you think? You can write *and* fight with it."

"Well, the pen *is* mightier than the sword." Diana laughed.

"Think you could teach me a thing or two about how to use it?" Sakina asked. "I got it right before we left."

"I'd love to," Diana said. She looked at Sakina's weapon and then at her friend. "I can't believe it's been a whole year since we last saw each other."

"Tell me about it. And look at you. You haven't changed a bit!"

But you have, Diana realized with a start. They'd always been about the same height, but standing next to her now, Diana saw that Sakina had shot up since their last meeting. She was a half foot taller than Diana. Her dark curls, which fell below her chin last summer, were braided down to her waist. Her tanned arms looked unmistakably muscled. Diana glanced down at her own skinny arms—between the two of them, people could mistake which one descended from warriors.

Something soft brushed against Diana's leg.

"Whoa!" She jumped back.

"Sorry! It's just silly Arya," Sakina said. "She's really into the element of surprise lately."

"This is your kitty?" Diana looked at the spotted snow leopard and petted her gently. The cat came up to Diana's hip. "I could scoop her up with one hand last summer."

"They grow superfast, but she's as much a cuddle bug as she ever was." Sakina looked around. "Is Binti nearby? Arya's been asking about her since we left. They had so much fun together last summer."

"She had babies," Diana said, warming at the thought of her wolf companion and her pups. "She's resting up."

"Babies!" Sakina's eyes lit up.

"They're the cutest wolf pups ever," Diana said. A thought occurred to her. Sakina was a Scholar, but she also had a special ability to speak with animals. "Actually, Binti's been acting strange the past few days. Maybe you can chat with her and see what's going on?"

"Sakina the animal whisperer at your service." She winked and curtseyed.

Suddenly the snow leopard froze. Her ears

pressed flat against her head. Narrowing her eyes, she raised her tail in the air and growled.

"Binti's not the only one acting strange." Sakina rolled her eyes. "Easy, Arya. You seriously need to relax."

The cat turned to Sakina and rumbled a deep-throated growl.

"What's the matter?" Diana asked. Goose bumps suddenly trailed her arms. She watched the animal's tense expression.

"Don't get me started." Sakina shook her head. "She was fine when we left, but mid-voyage she got all riled up. Snarling and growling at thin air. All cats are little divas, but Arya is the queen of them all."

"What's she been saying?" Diana asked.

"She's mad about the ships en route with us to your land," Sakina said. "Kept saying they're following us. Of course they're following us! I know it's strange to see a line of ships heading in one direction out on the open seas, but we're all using the same special coordinates to find Themyscira."

"Sorry, Arya," Diana apologized to the animal. "Nobody likes to feel like they're being followed."

Arya circled the girls. Diana studied the animal's raised hackles and the hard look in her eyes. Following the animal's gaze to the docked ships, a chill passed through Diana. Ever since she was young, Diana felt connected to animals. And though she couldn't put it into words, Arya's distress seemed deeper than the ships that followed them here. What exactly did the snow leopard think she saw?

"Princess Diana, dear!" Sakina's mother, Queen Khadijah, approached them. "So lovely to see you." She kissed Diana's cheek. The queen wore a cream-colored gown with flowers embroidered along the hem. Mira fluttered alongside her and landed on Sakina's shoulder.

"Wonderful to see you as well, Your Majesty," Diana said.

"Excited for your week together?" she asked the girls.

"We are." Sakina nodded. "And are you ready for all your boring meetings?"

"In due time." Her mother smiled. "Tonight we rest and enjoy; tomorrow we work. Has Arya calmed down at all?"

"Not really." Sakina shook her head. "She's still acting like there's a monster about to swoop down any minute."

"She'll adjust," her mother said. "There *are* quite a lot of new people here."

Indeed, more and more people filled the island, walking down long gangplanks from the newly docked ships. They hoisted banners and carried trunks and carts filled with goods from their homelands.

"You know how protective she's always been," Diana added as they began walking toward the main festival site. "Even as a kitten she loved to guard you."

"You have no idea. She's totally out of control now," Sakina groaned. "Ever since I started apprenticing at the library, she refuses to let me go alone. So now I have a huge cat prowling past the periodicals to protect me from dust mites."

"She just loves you," the queen said.

"She's not even as fierce as she thinks," Sakina said. "Half the time she's snoring by the sunny window near the reference desk."

"You're working at the library?" Diana stared at Sakina.

"Yes, I was going to tell you all about it! Can you believe it?" Sakina grinned.

"That's . . . that's wonderful," Diana managed to say. She was happy for her friend, truly. Sakina had wanted to apprentice at the library for as long as Diana could remember. Over the years they'd spent countless nights sharing their frustrations about not being able to do the things they loved most.

"She was after me about it for quite some time," her mother said. "I finally decided to let her try it so she could see how boring the work truly is. But I must hand it to her; she's taken to it well. She's a natural."

A natural.

Diana's throat constricted. Was this a part of her mother's hesitation with letting her train? Maybe her mother was trying to find a way to tell Diana there was no need for her to learn because *she* wasn't a natural fighter at all.

Diana glanced at the tents around her. Women set down sculpted vases and painted bowls. Silk dresses hung from hooks and fluttered in the breeze. Diana couldn't sculpt. She couldn't paint. She was not able to heal people with her words or with herbs. The one thing she wanted to do was be a true warrior, like the legendary Amazon warriors she lived alongside.

That was who she had always believed she was meant to be.

But now, with a sinking heart, Diana wondered if maybe she was wrong.

Chapter Two

The palace vibrated with the steady hum of laughter and conversation well into the evening. Dinner had just concluded, and lively music flowed through the expansive guest hall. Some women danced while others reclined on velvet sofas, sipping from glass goblets. A few stood by the floor-to-ceiling windows, gazing out at the waterfalls and flowering cliffsides; the scenery shone under the moonlit sky.

Taking the steps two at a time with Arya close at their heels, Diana and Sakina headed upstairs. From the landing above, the marble corridors of the palace stretched in multiple directions toward the palace baths as well as the many different living quarters and suites. Turning right, Diana headed to her bedroom and turned the handle.

Diana's bedroom was a large space with three windows overlooking the wooded grounds that stretched toward the craggy seaside cliffs. The mahogany shelves lining one of the walls were bursting with books—many of which Sakina had gifted to her over the years. Floating shelves on the opposite wall held trinkets and works of art.

"Have I told you how much I love this rug?" Sakina asked. She hopped onto the plush cream carpet in the center of the room. "Ah!" She twirled around, her braid spinning behind her. "Now *this* is what it would feel like to dance on a cloud."

"Do you want to share rooms again this year?" Diana asked her. "The guest room is set up if you'd rather have your own space."

"Seriously?" Sakina said. "We have to share a room, because sharing a room—"

"Maximizes our time together," the girls said in unison.

Diana laughed. They had this conversation every year.

Mira fluttered into the room and perched on the middle windowsill. She tapped her golden beak against the window and blinked at the girls before turning her head and sending bolts of light from her eyes into the darkness.

"Does she want to go outside?" Diana asked. "Sinla and Jasnin will be excited to see her again!"

"Not as excited as Mira. She can't get enough of the winged horses on Themyscira," Sakina said. She leaned over and unlatched the window, opening it. The bird fluttered outside. In an instant, Arya leapt up, her paws gripping the windowsill.

"Arya!" Sakina slammed the window shut. "No."

The snow leopard scraped at the glass urgently with her paw and moaned.

"What's she saying?" Diana asked.

"She's being ridiculous." Sakina rolled her eyes. "Keeps saying 'they're here' over and over again. *Of course* everyone is here."

The cat chuffed. Her gaze remained fixed toward the docks.

"I'm sorry. I know you want to explore, but you can't go off wandering alone. Not with the way you're acting," Sakina said. "Maybe tomorrow, once you've calmed down."

"I know how she feels," Diana said, remembering her conversation with her mother from earlier in the day. "I've been feeling a bit cooped up myself lately."

"Wait." Sakina looked at her. "Has your mother seriously still not budged on letting you train?"

"Not even a little bit." Diana shook her head. "I feel a little stuck lately."

"I get it. I feel that way, too, sometimes."

"You?" Diana asked. "But you're apprenticing at the library. It's what you've always dreamed of."

"I didn't tell you what my apprenticeship was." She smiled bashfully. "It's not like I'm inputting information or curating books or even organizing the collections. I'm . . . dusting."

"Dusting?"

"Yep. Literally dusting books. We have so many titles, they require constant upkeep. I clean the spines and bookshelves and make sure the pages are intact. Pretty impressive, don't you think?"

"Well . . ." Diana's voice trailed off.

"I mean, fine. Okay. It's important work. Whatever." Sakina flopped backward onto Diana's bed. "But this wasn't exactly what I had in mind when I begged my mother to let me apprentice. I thought I'd at least get to observe the curating process or trail one of our book detectives who locate rare books around the world. But no. I'm wandering through bookshelves with a duster and a snow leopard by my side. I began at the *A*s three months ago and only last week worked my way to the *D*s. At this rate, I'll finish the *Z*s when I'm twenty and will have to go back to start all over again."

Sakina had a point. It didn't sound like much fun to wipe down books for hours, but at least she was *there.* She was on the brink of the journey she'd always dreamed of instead of watching wistfully from the sidelines. It was more than what Diana could say for herself.

"I'm sure once they see how well you're doing, they'll move you up to other more interesting things," said Diana, settling down on the bed next to her. "It's only a matter of time."

"I hope so. And to be fair, it's not all bad." Sakina

sat up and shrugged. "I get to read while I dust, which is pretty nice. I've learned so much—random things that'll be of no use, but it's still interesting to learn about the history of alligators, the different types of bears, and the workings of clocks. The *D* section is more interesting than I'd realized. Long-forgotten demons. Dragons, real and fictional. Can't wait until I move on to the *Es*," she said with a wink. "Maybe I'll discover the evolution of eggs or something."

"You're lucky to have so many books at your disposal," Diana said. They had their own impressive library at Themyscira across from the white-walled armory, but it couldn't compete with the kingdom that hosted the largest libraries in the world.

"Oh!" Sakina's eyes lit up. "I almost forgot!" She hurried to her belongings tucked in the corner of the room and opened a leather bag. "Brought these for you." She balanced a heap of books in her arms and walked over to Diana.

"Did you find it?" Diana exclaimed. "The book about eastern swords?"

"Um—what kinda friend would I be if I didn't?"

Sakina said. She set the tower of books on the nightstand.

Swords of the East lay on the very top of the pile. Diana skimmed the spines, which mentioned ancient warriors and galaxies and worlds beyond Earth's horizon.

"These are perfect," Diana said. "You're incredible."

"I agree. I am pretty incredible." Sakina grinned and pretended to bow.

The citrusy scent of lemon wafted into their room.

"Mmm." Diana's eyes lit up. "Thelma must have made her famous upside-down lemon cake. One bite and you're going to think you've died and gone to heaven."

"Yum! Sounds like my kind of cake," Sakina said. The girls bounded up and out of Diana's room and toward the celebration.

Inside the guest hall, the music had shifted to a more up-tempo beat. Lights twinkled overhead as the marble dance floor quickly filled. Aunt Antiope twirled a guest, the woman's lavender dress fanning out into a circle. Diana smiled. All the women on the island had worked long hours to set up the festival. It was nice to see everyone relax.

"Sakina," Queen Khadijah called out. She sat on a velvet sofa by the rear guest doors and waved her daughter over. "I need you for a quick second."

Suddenly Diana paused.

Binti!

In all the excitement, she'd forgotten about the wolf and her pups. They were camped out in the forest not far from the palace walls. Diana had tried coaxing Binti out of her cramped burrow so she could recover at the palace like she normally did, but the animal refused to budge this time.

"I'll be back in a second. I need to get Binti something to eat," Diana told Sakina.

"I want to see her!" Sakina's eyes widened. "I'll meet up with you outside when I'm done."

The kitchen was full. Women washed dishes while others cut the lemon cake and placed slices on porcelain plates for servers to whisk away to the guests. Others stood by the stove, chopping strawberries and coring pineapples for breakfast the next morning.

Diana poked her head into the pantry, sifting through the radishes and cabbages.

"Heading off to see Binti?" Thelma, the head chef, asked.

"Yes. Any leftovers you think she might eat?"

"I packed her a leg of lamb." Thelma pointed to a paper-wrapped box on the counter. "Think she'll like it?"

"Like it? That's her favorite!"

Diana tucked the package under her arm and filled a metal bowl with water before pushing open the back doors of the palace. They spilled onto a path leading straight into the forest.

Other than the sound of the wind whistling through the trees, it was silent as she stepped onto the palace grounds. Her thoughts drifted to her conversation with her mother. Were her private fears true? Did her own mother think she couldn't handle being a warrior? Diana thought back to all the times she'd snuck into trainings in the coliseum. Just last week she'd trapped Lena, one of the most experienced fighters on the island, into a headlock during a self-defense training session. But now Diana wondered—had Lena *pretended* to lose? Diana *was* a princess, after all, so did the Amazon warriors *let* her win because they had to?

Arriving at a towering grove of sequoia trees, Diana peeked into the wolf's burrow, which was tucked within a hollowed-out trunk.

"Hey, Binti," Diana said softly.

The four pups looked sweet as ever—each one was uniformly gray with white stripes along its nose, like their mother. Their eyes still firmly shut, they clung close to Binti for warmth.

"Thelma packed you a nice big leg of lamb," Diana said, unwrapping the meat. "And here's a bowl of water for you."

The wolf opened her green eyes and looked at the food. Then she lowered her head to the ground.

"What's the matter?" Diana asked. The wolf hadn't eaten since she'd given birth; surely she was famished. "Not in the mood for lamb? I can get you something else. . . ." The wolf moved her foot toward Diana and whimpered. Diana gasped. "Oh,

Binti." Her left paw was swollen and red.

"Is this why you didn't come to the palace with me?" Diana asked. "This looks like an infection. But don't worry, there are healers here, the best in the world. And Sakina's here, too. We'll get you and your pups the help you need."

The wolf nuzzled Diana's hand.

"I'll be right back," she promised.

Hurrying through the woods, Diana had just stepped into the clearing toward home when a distant high-pitched noise echoed through the island.

What was that? Diana strained her ears, but the sound had vanished.

Maybe I'm hearing things, thought Diana. Or perhaps the noise had escaped from the window of a guest suite left open in the palace.

As she took another step toward home, the noise returned, followed by a scraping sound. It echoed from across the forest. Diana tensed. No animals on the island made noises like that, and everyone else was inside the palace.

Diana glanced into the darkness, debating what to do. It was probably nothing more than a tree creaking in the breeze. But before she could take another step, a howling scream pierced the sky.

Diana's heart skipped a beat. This was definitely not a something, but a *someone.* Her hand firmly on her sword, she inched toward the sound.

"Help!" a voice cried out. "Someone. Please help me!"

Diana picked up her pace. Worry hammering in her chest, she hurried past the grassy coliseum toward the ships. The sound seemed to be coming from that direction. Her feet skidded on the rocky paths leading to the docks. She stopped in place and listened, eyes scanning the scene—but nothing seemed amiss.

Then she looked up.

Diana froze.

There it was. A metallic ladder, propped precariously against a ship. And upon the ladder, wearing a torn shirt and dirt-encrusted pants, was the strangest sight she'd ever seen in her life.

A *boy.*

Chapter Three

No, it was a hallucination. It had to be.

But when Diana took another step closer—there it was.

Or rather, there *he* was.

Definitely a boy.

It made no sense. Males were not allowed on Themyscira. There were few rules as ironclad as this.

The boy stood hunched precariously on the top rung of the ladder, his body contorted into an awkward position. Taking a step closer, she saw that his shirtsleeve was caught on a thick nail protruding from the ship. He swung his arm back and forth furiously but seemed unable to unsnag his shirt—

the ladder wobbled dangerously as he swayed and struggled to free himself.

"Who are you?" Diana asked evenly, getting the boy's attention. He looked at her with a start.

"Is it—is it you?" he stammered. He stared at her as though he were seeing a ghost. "Are you Diana?"

Diana's eyes narrowed. Not only was there a boy on the island, but he also knew her name.

Drawing her sword, she took a determined step toward him.

"N-no! It's not what you think! I don't mean any harm!" The boy looked at the weapon in terror. Wincing, he forcefully yanked at his shirtsleeve until it finally tore loose from the nail. The ladder swayed. He reached out, his fingers trying to grasp the edge of the ship to steady himself. "I'm—I'm not—" His words died in his throat. The ladder jerked to the side violently. And then it began tipping backward. Free-falling away from the boat. It swung down like a hammer toward the dock.

He's going to fall to his death, Diana realized with horror. She stuffed her sword into her belt and rushed toward him. She had to stop the ladder from hitting the ground. Pumping her arms, her feet flew so fast they barely seemed to touch the ground. The scenery passed by in a blur. In a flash, Diana shot out a hand and gripped the ladder's edge. Clenching her jaw, she locked her arm, holding it in place at an angle. The boy hung from the top rung, his feet hovering inches from the dock.

"Jump!" she shouted, her fingers growing numb. "Now!"

The boy dropped to the ground and hurried out of the ladder's path. Gently, Diana lowered it until it rested on the dock. She exhaled, willing her wild heartbeat to calm itself.

"Y-you saved my life," the boy said in a rush, walking toward her. "I've never seen anyone run so fast. It was . . . incredible. Thank you."

"You're welcome," she replied. "Now I need . . ."

Her voice trailed off. A boy—a real live *boy*—was standing on the docks of Themyscira. She studied him carefully. He looked to be about her age; they were the same height. He had scruffy blond hair and green eyes peering at her through silver wire-rimmed eyeglasses. Bruises and scrapes trailed his arms and face. His shirtsleeve, torn through from the jagged nail, was speckled with blood.

"You're injured." She took a step toward him.

"No—it's okay. I'm fine. Just clumsy is all. Was trying to get down from the ship and slipped a little. Sleeve got stuck. It happens." The boy stood up straighter—and then he clutched his arm.

"You don't look fine to me."

"It's a scrape," he said through clenched teeth. "I get scrapes all the time."

Diana pictured Binti's paw. "Even a scrape can grow deadly if it's not treated properly. May I see? If you don't mind."

The boy bit his lip and rolled up his sleeve. His entire elbow was bloodied.

Diana gasped. "You've got a gash. It's still bleeding. I have salve and bandages back at the palace. I'm sure someone there can help you and . . ."

Diana swallowed. It was one thing to offer to help him, but how exactly would she transport a *boy* to the palace? And what would happen to him when he turned up? The idea of a male arriving at Themyscira had always seemed so impossible, she'd never considered it until now. But judging from the way he grimaced and clutched his elbow, he was injured enough to need the help of a healer.

"Oh n-n-no. There's no need. Really." The boy shook his head. "Haven't had a second to treat it is all. Skin punctures are routine—nothing to worry about. If it was a ligament or a fracture, I'd know it. This is a simple fix."

He lifted his shirt, revealing a leather pouch with numerous small compartments strapped to his waist. Opening one of the smaller pockets, he pulled out a roll of white gauze and expertly got to work, cleaning the wound and wrapping the gauze around his elbow. Poking around in the pack, he pulled out a glass vial with clear liquid and drank it in one gulp.

"There," he said. "I'll be good as new soon."

"What did you just drink?" Diana asked curiously.

"A healing potion," he said. "When you're as clumsy as I am, you make sure never to leave home without one. Cures you from the inside out." He smiled a little. The first smile since they'd met. "Came up with this one myself."

"*You* made it?"

"It was simple to compound," he said. "People think it's complicated to come up with new cures, but if you're willing to experiment and fail a few times, sooner or later you'll stumble onto a clue that you're on the right track, and then, well, you can really invent or discover something truly exceptional."

"So you're a potion maker."

"Kind of." His smile faded. He pushed his glasses up the bridge of his nose. "I don't really get a chance to do it as much as I'd like these days."

Waves crashed against the darkened cliffs in the distance. Diana's mind raced with questions. But one question needed answering before anything else.

"You know my name," she said. "But who are *you*?"

The boy's expression fell. He glanced at the ocean and then at the ship his ladder was hoisted upon before it tipped backward. Diana followed his gaze. The mast with the quill and scroll.

"Are you with the *Scholars*?" she asked.

He hesitated a moment. Then, slowly, he nodded.

This explained how he knew her name. But—

"Sakina's my best friend. She never mentioned you," Diana said. "Males aren't allowed on our island. It's a rule everyone agrees to before they are given our coordinates."

"I'm so, so sorry," he said quickly. "I didn't know those rules. It's not like anyone tells the servant about such things. I go where they tell me to. I've . . . I've learned not to ask questions."

"Servant?" she repeated. "Whose? Sakina doesn't have servants. Are you the queen's servant?"

The boy bit his lip before nodding.

"But they didn't bring any servants on this voyage," she said. "Every captain must disclose the contents aboard their ship and the passengers on their manifest when they dock."

"Guess I wasn't on the manifest," the boy said softly.

Diana frowned. The Scholars had been part of the Chará festival since the early days. They were among its original founders. They knew better than most the rules of Themyscira. And they certainly knew how serious a breach of rules it was to bring a boy to the island. Diana rested her hands on her hips and studied the boy's solemn expression.

"I was told to stay in the hull and out of sight." He looked at the ground. His voice wavered. "They must have known I shouldn't be seen. . . . I'm just so hungry. I wanted to see if I could scrounge something up."

"Are you saying Queen Khadijah left you on a ship without food or water?"

The boy hesitated before nodding.

Diana shook her head. "That makes no sense."

"Y-you don't know her like I do. The queen—she was angry with m-me." The boy's voice trembled. "I ironed her clothes, but I didn't get the edges right. When she gets upset, she does things most people would never imagine doing—many things I wish she wouldn't. You don't want to see her when she gets upset."

"Impossible," Diana said firmly. "She would never . . ."

But her voice trailed off when she looked at the

scrapes and bruises along his arms and face. Her stomach turned.

"Are you saying Sakina's mother did that?"

"I'm . . . I'm sorry," he said. "I can see that you think well of her."

Diana's head hurt. She'd known the queen all her life and she'd never so much as raised her voice to anyone. And then there was the other matter: If what the boy said was true, why hadn't Sakina stopped her mother?

"Diana!" a voice called in the distance.

It was Sakina. Diana exhaled. Finally she could get an explanation.

"Well, there's Sakina now." Diana turned away from the boy and glanced at the forest. "Let's talk to her and sort this out."

"N-no. She can't know you saw me!" The boy winced, gripping his elbow. "Please."

"You don't have to fear Sakina. She won't do anything to you."

"She won't d-do *anything.* No one d-does anything when I bear the worst of her mother's fury.

Please. If you call out for her, if she sees me here talking to you"—the boy shuddered—"I'll be done for."

Diana's head spun. It was impossible to believe such a thing, but here was a boy on her island with scrapes across his arms and face, shaking like a sheet of paper in the wind at the sound of Sakina's voice.

"Diana! Where'd you go?" Sakina's voice sounded in the forest.

"Diana," he begged her. His eyes grew moist. "You would never let anyone get hurt. Would you?"

"Of course not," Diana said. "But—"

"The way you rushed to save me from the falling ladder . . . You are good and kind. Please promise you won't say anything. At least not until we have a chance to talk more. My life is in danger. I'm begging you. Promise you'll wait until I can explain." Tears streamed down his face. "Please!"

"Diana! Are you okay?" Sakina's voice called out.

Sakina was close. She'd find them by the docks in a minute. Diana hesitated. Asking Sakina would clear this all up in a matter of seconds. The boy's story didn't make sense. But what if he *was* telling the truth? What would Queen Khadijah do?

Maybe I can talk to my mother, Diana thought. But what would happen to the boy if he were found out? Males weren't allowed. Diana studied the boy's stricken face—could she live with herself if the consequences were worse than she could imagine?

"Fine!" Diana finally said. "I'll come back later tonight. You can tell me everything then. Until I return and get some answers from you, I promise I won't say anything."

She hurried into the woods behind the docks, following Sakina's calls.

"Here!" Diana shouted once she was far enough away from the ships. "I'm by the chestnut trees!"

"There you are! I was starting to think you got kidnapped by aliens," Sakina exclaimed. She parted a field of bamboo in the forest's center and walked over to her. "Binti's all the way out here?"

"Not too far from here," Diana said. "Come, I'll show you."

They walked toward the towering sequoia trees.

The moon shone full and bright upon the land. Diana looked at her friend. She longed to ask Sakina about the boy, but Diana had promised she'd let him explain first. And though Diana never broke her word, the thought of having to keep something—especially something so monumental—from her best friend made her feel sick with betrayal.

Binti whimpered when they reached the clearing.

"Yikes! That looks painful!" Sakina said when she saw the wolf. "When did it happen?"

The wolf howled a response.

"Two days ago? And it's getting worse and worse, huh? Mind if I take a peek?"

The wolf rested her paw in front of Sakina, who traced her hand across it. Binti pulled back and howled.

"That's a splinter," Sakina said. "Looks like it got wedged in a tricky place. Can I take it out? Might hurt for a second, but then it'll be over."

The wolf buried her head in her forearms and whimpered.

"One. Two . . . and three." Sakina's face flushed as

she squeezed, and then she yanked out the splinter. "There. All done."

Binti licked her paw. Then she leapt up and licked Sakina's face with gratitude.

"Happy to help." Sakina laughed. "You'll be completely better soon enough. Look at this." She turned to Diana, holding up the scraggly thorn. "Such a tiny thing causing so much pain."

"I don't know how I missed it," Diana said, shaking her head.

"The same thing happened with Mira," Sakina said. "She belonged to a merchant in town. He kept her locked in a cage, and she screeched loudly every single day. I finally marched over and demanded to see what the matter was. Turned out a shard of glass was buried deep in her claw. He never bothered to check. I paid him a price he couldn't refuse. Even though I freed her, she decided to stick around."

This was the Sakina that Diana knew. How could the kind of person who stood up for an injured, trapped bird not stand up for her mother's mistreated servant?

"You must have been upset someone would hurt

a living thing like that," Diana said cautiously.

"You have no idea." Sakina's expression darkened at the memory. "My mother was even more furious. Trust me, you do not want to mess with her when she gets angry."

Diana winced, thinking of what the boy had said. So it was true—Sakina's mother did have a temper. But it was one thing to lash out at a brutish vendor and another to harm a boy. And to leave him alone on a ship without water or food? That wasn't just mean; it was *cruel.*

Diana wondered if her friend knew how badly the boy had been treated. There was no way she could have known and not acted upon it. Sakina would never stand by in the face of injustice. The boy was wrong about this. He had to be. Diana bit her lip. It was as simple as asking her friend a question. Some clarity was all she needed. She'd promised the boy she wouldn't say anything, but this promise was proving harder and harder to keep.

Back at the palace, Sakina and Diana sat under a patio awning. Leafy grapevines wound around the trellises above them, enveloping them in a canopy outside the guest hall. A chessboard rested on the table between them.

"Boom!" Sakina set her pawn down across from Diana's knight with a dramatic flourish. "You watch. This little pawn is going to take you down, Diana!"

Diana turned her bishop to the right and tapped her foot impatiently. It had been three hours since she'd seen the boy. She'd hoped that by now everyone would start retiring for the evening and she could bring him something to eat and drink, but through the glass windows of the guest hall, the lights twinkled just as bright. Though some women yawned, the party showed no signs of winding down. The Amazons danced and conversed animatedly among their visitors.

"Look who's beating you at your favorite game today," Sakina said, knocking down Diana's knight. "You are not bringing your best self tonight."

"I'm tired." Diana swallowed and fixed her eyes on the game board.

"Tired? It's not even midnight yet. We usually stay up until the sun comes up on my first night here. I was hoping, after this game, we could head to the royal stables to ride the Sky Kangas like last summer."

"Maybe tomorrow. It's been a long day," Diana said tersely.

"All right," Sakina said suddenly. "Out with it." She leaned back in her cushioned seat and crossed her arms. "What's with you?"

"Am I not allowed to get tired?" Diana asked pointedly.

"That's not what I meant," Sakina said. "You've been acting different ever since we got back from seeing Binti. You know you can tell me anything."

"It's nothing. I'm tired. I think I need to get some rest." Diana stood up. "I'll see you in the morning."

Before Sakina could respond, Diana opened the patio doors, hurried through the guest hall, and entered the kitchen. She pushed away the pinprick of guilt at the thought of the hurt look on her friend's face. She'd never been short with Sakina before. But she needed to get to the bottom of what was going on. The sooner the better.

The kitchen was empty when she stepped inside. Diana grabbed everything she needed—a container of lamb and vegetables, leftover bread, and a jug of water. She scanned the kitchen to make sure no one was watching her and then slipped out the back door.

It took Diana a while to find the boy. He sat on the dock, concealed partly by the hull of the Scholars' ship. His feet dangled inches above the water.

"Careful!" Diana quickly called out. "There's a herd of megalodon sharks that likes to hang out near the docks. They can jump pretty high when they're hungry."

The boy startled and turned around. His glasses slid down his nose. He hopped to his feet.

"Y-you're here," he stammered.

"I'm sorry it got late. This is a busy week." She handed him the food and water.

The boy sat cross-legged on the dock and, in a matter of minutes, devoured everything. He gulped the jug of water down in three swallows. *It looks like he was definitely telling the truth about how hungry he was,* thought Diana.

"I can get you more," she said once the boy finished.

"This is enough. More than enough." He wiped his mouth with his torn sleeve. "The lamb was exquisite—roasted to perfection. They must have cooked it on low heat. It's what I do when I need to draw out flavor from the herbs I work with, and . . ." His voice trailed off. He blushed. "Sorry, I get caught up on the properties of things, food or otherwise. Thank you. I hadn't eaten in some time."

"So," Diana said. She sat down next to the boy. "You know my name. But I don't know yours."

"Oh, right." The boy's smile faltered. "My name is Augustus."

"Augustus," Diana repeated. "It's a nice name. Not from the Scholar community, though, is it?"

"Oh yes. I mean no. You're right. I'm originally from Sáz. My family is . . . They're poor. I work as a servant, and that way I c-can send money home."

"It must be awful to live so far from your family."

"It's honest work, and, well, we need it. Besides, it

could be worse," the boy said. He studied the ground.

"I've heard of your lands," Diana said. "You build chariots for the gods, don't you?"

"Yes!" He nodded. "We make brilliant chariots. All sorts. For parades and festivities and for the more practical ruling needs the gods may have. It's our specialty."

"And you make potions in your spare time?"

"Chariot making runs through my blood, but it gets dull sometimes. There are only so many different ways to make them. Sáz sits on a former volcano, and the area is rich in plants and minerals—perfect for potion making. Mr. Broderick, our town's apothecary, let me study under him and learn how to make them. Mr. Broderick says—I mean . . . he *said*—back when I lived on Sáz, that I have a real knack for it."

"Must be nice. To be gifted at something," Diana said. She wasn't sure if she could say the same for herself.

The boy looked up at her then.

"Sáz isn't too far away," he said. "I brought a

chariot with me. Uh, snuck it in the hull so no one would discover it. Thought I'd visit my family while I was here."

"It can fly all on its own?"

"With a certain potion, yes." He patted his pocket. He looked at her and hesitated. "I'd love to take you to Sáz and show you around tonight, if you're interested."

"Tonight?"

"You'd love it," he said quickly. "I think it's statistically impossible for anyone not to."

"Oh. Well . . ." Diana blinked at the unexpected invitation.

"There are rubies and other gems there," he said, nodding to the emerald-decorated sword tucked into her belt. "You have some lovely waterfalls here—more than I've ever seen in one spot before—but we have interesting natural formations and sights back at Sáz. And the chariot can fly exceptionally high with my newest potion. Would be fun to fly above the clouds, wouldn't it? I could have you back by morning."

Earlier this evening she'd told Sakina how stuck she felt. Now here was a boy offering her a trip to a brand-new land and urging her to join him.

It was tempting.

"I'd love to," she finally said. "But this is a busy week. I can't worry my mother by disappearing on her."

"Oh," Augustus said. His expression fell. "Well . . ."

"But you should go. If I see any of the Scholars heading over to the ship, I'll distract them. They won't notice you're gone."

"Thank you. Maybe tomorrow evening, then," he said. "My injuries should be fully healed by then."

Diana told Augustus she'd check on him the next morning. She promised to drop by with breakfast and freshly squeezed orange juice.

"Thank you," said Augustus.

"It's not a problem," she said. "Really."

"Well, thank you all the same. For your kindness. Been a while since I was shown any."

Diana studied the boy's face, his pained expression. Stepping off the dock, she headed toward the forest. Her cheeks burned with frustration. If Queen Khadijah took a boy so young as her servant and treated him badly, why didn't Sakina stop her?

She needed answers.

Suddenly Diana stopped walking.

The Lasso of Truth. It was the one object that drew out the truth, no matter what.

Quickly, Diana turned from the palace. She hurried through the coliseum instead, racing past the empty seats and the rose gardens.

She headed straight toward the armory.

It was time to ask some hard questions. With the Lasso of Truth, she'd get to the bottom of things once and for all. Queen Hippolyta definitely would not approve of Diana removing the lasso from the armory without permission, but if she used it on Sakina or her mother, it would reveal all without leaving any room for doubt. Diana needed to know if Augustus was telling her the truth.

His life could depend on it.

Chapter Four

The white walls of the armory loomed in the distance. Diana hurried toward its nasturtium-lined entrance and turned the door handle. All along the armory's inside perimeter hung the rarest of weapons and swords. Warm torchlight shone down upon them; placards beneath each one signified their importance. Diana could lose herself within the armory most days; there was so much to see and try out. But tonight was different. She was here for exactly one thing.

And there it was.

The Lasso of Truth glimmered beneath the torchlights across from her. Walking up to it, she hesitated. It's not that she'd never handled the lasso.

She'd run her hands over the intricate knotting in the past when no one was looking. But those times didn't count. Not really. She'd never used the lasso on someone to find out a necessary truth. And she never could have imagined she'd ever need to use this lasso on her best friend.

Diana lifted the lasso from its perch. It looked like any ordinary rope, but as soon as her hands touched it, the thick lasso began to glow. She glanced down at it and hesitated. She was allowed to wander the armory and explore as she liked, but her mother would *not* be happy if she found out Diana had removed the lasso from the armory without asking first—and to use it on one of their closest allies! But the Lasso of Truth was a source of answers, and answers were what she desperately needed. She tied the lasso to her waist belt and vowed to be as careful as possible with the rare heirloom before she walked out of the armory and back into the night.

As she entered the palace, Diana paused in the gleaming marble foyer. The strangest thing echoed through the normally bustling palace: *silence.* A short while ago, every inch of this place had been brimming with music and laughter and conversation. It was too soon for *everyone* to have retired to their rooms for bed, but maybe she'd caught a lucky break. If Sakina was asleep, it would be the most painless way to get the truth out of her. But when Diana went to her bedroom, both beds were still perfectly made. Sakina wasn't there.

Diana poked her head out of the room and scanned the corridor. The doors to the guest suites were opened wide. She passed each of them and saw that they were empty. Every last one.

Where is everyone?

Diana hurried downstairs toward the guest hall. Maybe they were still there. Sure, she'd never heard it this quiet during a Chará festival, but perhaps they were playing some kind of game. Or meditating. It was a little late for such things, but odder things had happened at festivals past.

She gripped the handle to the guest hall door and glanced at the lasso at her waist. It was too big to tuck under her clothes and too important to let out of her sight, but if she ran into her mother with it attached to her waist, she would be in big trouble.

Best to avoid her mother as best she could, Diana resolved.

The first thing Diana noticed once she stepped inside the guest hall was the scent filling the room: bittersweet, like the rind of an orange. She clasped a hand to her nose; her eyes watered. Glancing around the room, her arms fell to her sides.

She was dreaming.

She had to be.

All the women were here.

Every last one.

Their eyes were closed. And none of them were moving.

Chapter Five

Diana wheeled around and stared at the women surrounding her. Her stomach twisted in knots. They were here, just as she'd left them. Except now, besides the light movements of their breath, none of them moved a muscle. A woman in a chiffon dress sat across from her, perched in a high-backed chair, her eyes gently shut as though in deep meditation. Another sat by the window, her cheek pressed against the smooth glass, her eyes closed. How had everyone fallen asleep so suddenly?

"Hello?" Diana called out, her own breathing growing more rapid. "Can you hear me? Can *anyone* hear me?"

No one responded. The candlelit chandeliers

shone brightly overhead as dread filled Diana's heart.

Queen Khadijah sat on a velvet sofa, her hands clasped primly in her lap. Her eyes were shut. All around her, motionless women sat in chairs and reclined on chaise longues. Some were even asleep on the cool marble floor.

Diana startled when her eyes landed on her mother. She lay on a chaise longue by a window.

Seeing the queen's unconscious face, her hands limp at her sides, Diana's chest filled with a new fear.

What if all the women weren't sleeping? What if some of them were . . .

Rushing to her mother, Diana pressed her fingers against Queen Hippolyta's wrist. To her relief, her mother's pulse beat steady and strong.

"Mother? Wake up." Diana squeezed her mother's arm and clasped her face with her hands. "The palace is on fire! The armory, too! And I lost your crown!"

Diana swallowed. Her mother didn't move. She didn't respond at all.

"Mother!" Diana's pleas grew more frantic. "Please wake up. There's something important I need to tell you. It's an emergency."

But none of her words got through. The queen's expression remained peaceful and unchanged. Panic bubbled inside Diana. She pushed back tears. Even if they did not see eye to eye on all matters, her mother was the one person who helped everything make sense—who righted wrongs and brought back order if things were getting out of control. How was Diana going to fix any of this without her?

Dashing into the kitchen, Diana drew a sharp intake of breath; the scene was the same as in the guest hall. Thelma was slumped over the sink, a porcelain dish and sponge still in her hands. Two other cooks were sprawled and snoring on the marble kitchen floor. The same bitter smell of orange rinds clung thick to the air.

Diana breathlessly raced into each of the palace rooms. She checked the closets, the solarium, the bathing rooms. There had to be an explanation. A palace of people didn't pass out at the same time, without any reason. Something—*someone*—did this to them. Someone attacked the palace. Someone tried to hurt Diana's family and friends—*oh!*

The thought jolted her. There was one person still unaccounted for: Sakina. Where was Sakina?

Hurrying into the darkness outside the palace, Diana raced down the sandy path and into the forest. She sped toward the burrow, but, save Binti and her sleeping babies, there was no one there.

"Sakina!" Diana called out. "We need to talk! Where are you?"

Sakina did not appear. But Mira did. Darts of silver light shot through the night sky. She fluttered her wings and approached Diana, chirping in a high-pitched squawk. Swooping down, the bird tugged Diana's sleeve. Diana understood.

"Light the way, Mira."

Diana raced behind the bird, clear to the other side of the trees. Stepping out of the woods, Diana looked around. They were not far from the docks. Mira flew toward the Scholars' ship.

Inching closer, she heard a deep growl. Diana's stomach sank. The sound meant only one thing.

Hurrying to the dock, Diana looked around—and paused. There she was. The snow leopard, crouched low and facing the boy. Even from fifty feet away, Diana could see the cat's sharp teeth bared at him. And next to the snow leopard stood Sakina. Her arms were crossed. Her back was to Diana.

Sweat dripped down Augustus's face. His cheeks were pink and flushed. His body was pressed against the side of the ship, leaning over the small gap of water between the dock's edge and the boat.

"I think your five minutes are up," Sakina said coolly to the boy. "So what's it going to be? If you can't do what I need you to do, then this conversation is over. And trust me, when I tell her I found you out here, you won't like what comes next."

Diana blinked back tears. So it was true? The boy had been telling the truth?

"P-please," the boy said with a trembling voice. "Don't hurt me."

"I won't lay a finger on you," Sakina replied. "But Arya could use a good meal."

Arya snarled and took a step forward.

Diana gasped. She'd known Arya since the snow

leopard was a tiny little thing. Around them she mostly acted like an overgrown kitty. Diana had forgotten how powerful the creature truly was. And judging from the way Arya glared at the boy, it looked like she *was* eager to eat him for dinner.

"Stop!" Diana cried out. "Arya! Don't do anything!"

Sakina turned to look at Diana.

"Diana." She frowned. "What are you doing here? Did Mira—"

But before Sakina could complete her sentence, Diana ran toward them. She leapt in front of Augustus, shielding him with her body.

"*What* are you doing?" asked Sakina.

"Don't hurt him," said Diana.

"Hurt him?"

"Yes. I think he's been through enough, don't you?" Diana asked, biting her lip.

"What are you even talking about?" Sakina put her hands on her hips. "Hurt him? Why would you think I'd do *anything* to him?"

"I heard you with my own ears. You told Arya to get him."

"That? I was only trying to scare him," she said. "You know Arya doesn't eat people."

"Fine. But you have to leave the boy alone," Diana entreated. "You and your mother can't continue mistreating him."

"*What?* Me and my mother?" Sakina repeated. She crossed her arms. "*What* exactly have we done to him?"

"He told me everything. About Queen Khadijah's angry side. I saw the bruises for myself. I still can't understand it. Did you not know? Because if you did know, why didn't you stop it from happening?"

Sakina looked at the boy and then at Diana.

"Is that what he said?" she finally asked. "That we treat him poorly?"

"Are you saying it's some sort of misunderstanding?" Diana's voice wavered. "Because, honestly, I would love for some sort of explanation to clear all of this up."

"Diana," Sakina said slowly, "I've never seen this boy before in my life."

Diana looked toward Augustus. He stood still as a windless night.

"I can explain everything," the boy finally said.

Diana just barely stopped herself from gasping. *Augustus* had lied to her?

"Is it true?" Diana asked him. "You really don't know Sakina?"

"M-maybe. Okay. Fine. Yes. It's kind of true," he said hesitantly.

"Kind of?" Diana took a step toward him. Her eyes narrowed. "It's either true or it isn't. Pick one."

"Well, *truth* can so often be a relative term. Though if we're sticking *strictly* to the facts, then I suppose, technically, we can unambiguously say it's . . . ah . . ."

"Augustus?" Diana put her hands on her hips. "Out with it."

"Okay. Fine! It's true. I don't know her!" He ran a hand through his hair and frantically looked at the two girls. "B-but I have a good reason for why I said I did! Give me a chance to explain. Please."

Diana's brows furrowed. If he wasn't with the Scholars, then how had he gotten here? How had he accessed the secret coordinates? Where had he come from?

"We're all ears," Sakina replied.

"Why in the world would you lie about something so serious?" Diana demanded. "I heard you before and you said . . ."

Her voice trailed off. She glanced at the pouch tied to his waist—the one with many different compartments that contained potions and ingredients. Realization dawned on her. She'd saved this boy's life from a falling ladder. She'd brought him food and water. And yet . . .

"You," she said, putting the pieces together. "You did it. Didn't you?"

"Did what?" Sakina asked.

"He enchanted all the women," Diana said. Her eyes remained fixed on the boy. Anger pulsed through her veins. This boy had attacked her *home.* He'd come here and hurt her people. Her hand lowered to grip the hilt of her sword.

"Enchanted?" Sakina said. "Is . . . is everyone okay?"

"Every last person at the palace is asleep," Diana responded, her gaze focused tightly on Augustus. "The cooks. The metal welders. The painters. Our mothers. They're all unconscious. It was *you.* But why? *What* are you doing here? What do you want?"

Augustus said nothing. And then his eyes narrowed.

Before Diana could move, he lunged toward her.

Chapter Six

In an instant, Arya snarled and leapt on top of Augustus. She toppled him to the ground and pinned him firmly with her paws.

"Ow!" he shouted. "No! Please! Get off me!"

Flattened against the dock, he struggled to move, but the snow leopard growled loudly until he grew still.

Anger flooded Diana's chest. The boy had lied to her. And worse—her cheeks burned—she'd believed him. Who *was* he? It was time for answers.

"Let him up, Arya," she said evenly. "I'm ready."

Arya reluctantly stepped to the side. Groaning, the boy rubbed his chest and stomach before standing up unsteadily.

"Listen. . . . I can explain," he said, his hands up, palms facing out.

"Yes, you definitely will." Diana gritted her teeth. "I'm going to make sure of it."

Before he could say anything more, she reached for the lasso. A flicker of doubt crossed her mind. She hoped it would work.

"No, wait!" he cried out as the lasso flew through the air.

But it was too late. The lasso wrapped itself around his body.

"Stop! Please!" He yanked at the material, prying the threads with his fingers, but the more he struggled, the tighter the lasso wound around him. "Let me go! What is this thing?"

"It shines a light on the truth. And you can't break free of it," Diana said. "May as well stop trying."

"What are you going to d-do?" His voice quavered.

"I am going to get some answers."

She pulled the glimmering rope firmly toward her until she and the boy stood face-to-face.

"Let's start with an easy question first," she said. "Who are you?"

"Augustus," he said in a shaky voice. "I'm Augustus Dimilio. I'm not a bad person. I swear. Please let me explain—"

"Why did you pretend to be a servant?"

"I'm—I'm sorry. I needed a cover. When you mentioned the name Sakina—how this ship here belonged to the Scholars—I made something up on the spot. I needed to hide out a bit. I had to buy time."

"How did you find our island?" Diana asked.

"He must have snuck on my ship," Sakina said.

"I flew here. On a chariot," he said. "I flew behind this ship. I hovered below the deck but just above the water to avoid being seen."

"Oh, Arya." Sakina swiveled to look at the cat. "Is this what you were trying to say? You weren't complaining about the ships following us. You were warning us about *him.*"

Arya rested her head against Sakina's leg and purred.

"What do you want? Why are you here?" Diana demanded.

The boy stopped struggling against the lasso. He hung his head.

"For you."

Me? Diana glanced at Sakina. She looked as shocked as Diana felt.

"I came on orders." Augustus's eyes grew moist. "I—I was told to follow a route of ships heading past our lands to this island. To find a girl named Diana and to bring her back as soon as I could."

"Why?"

"I can't. I can't tell you. I'm supposed to say as little as possible about my mission." Augustus struggled against the lasso again. His face flushed. He strained his arms against the restraint, trying to break free.

"He's going to kill them. My people." The boy finally sputtered. "Said he was going to destroy us all and burn my lands to the ground if I didn't succeed."

Diana's mouth went dry. A chill passed through her. Someone was threatening to *kill* people and destroy an entire nation just to get to her? Why was she so important? She hadn't even trained as a warrior. What could anyone want with her?

"Who is doing this? What's his name?" she asked.

"I don't know. Wish I d-did." Augustus's voice shook. "I'd never seen him before yesterday. He's . . . he's not like you and me. He's not human. Can't be, not with the way he moves. The things he's done."

Not human? The more questions she asked this boy, the more questions they brought forward.

"If he's not human, what is he? Are you saying he's a god?" Diana asked.

"Not a god. No way." The boy shook his head. "Our island nation builds chariots for the gods, and they in turn give us special protection. Whatever this thing is, it defies all scientific explanation. He looks solid enough at first glance, but it's like he's made of gas or vapors."

Sakina gasped. "A demon. I read about them a few days ago. I'm blanking on the type, but it's definitely a demon. It's got to be."

"What does a demon want with me?" Diana asked slowly.

"I don't know," Augustus said. His eyes grew wet

with tears. "But he's hypnotized everyone who lives on my land to get to you."

"Are *you* hypnotized?"

"It didn't work on me." He shook his head. "Not sure how. He spoke, but the words did nothing."

"Were your ears covered?" Sakina asked.

"Yes!" Augustus nodded as realization dawned. "I had Jika flower petals in my ears. They're soft like cotton and grow along the cliffsides. I use them to reduce noise so I can focus better on my potion making."

"I remember reading something like that in a passage about demons who use hypnosis," Sakina said excitedly. "People stuff their ears with cotton to block the effect."

"I guess the petals were effective enough, but when he threatened to kill everyone I know, he got me to work for him all the same."

Diana studied Augustus's stricken expression; the pain he felt was clear across his face. He'd been through a terrible ordeal—of that much she was certain.

"Is he the one who did this to you?" Diana pointed to the bruises and scrapes along his arms.

"His touch burns like fire," Augustus said softly.

"And they sent *you*?" Diana asked. "You look like you're the same age as me."

"He thought it would be the best way to earn your trust, figured that would be the easiest way to bring you back."

And it almost worked, Diana thought. Her cheeks burned.

"And the women you put to sleep," Diana asked. "Did you poison their drinks?"

"Never! I-it's nothing to worry about. They're asleep is all. All the herbs I used to blend are safe. I tested each ingredient myself."

"Why?" Diana demanded. "Why on earth would you want them asleep?"

"Wasn't meant for them," he said weakly. "It was for you. It's the misting potion of eternal sleep. It's a reputable potion. I got it from Mr. Broderick's own book. You were there when I released it. I thought for sure it would work, but . . . I don't know how to explain it. . . . It didn't have any effect on you at all."

Diana froze. *Eternal* meant forever. Which meant—

"Hold up a second. Are you saying they'll never wake up?" Sakina asked slowly.

"There's an antidote," he said quickly. "Mr. Broderick's potions always come with an antidote. It'll work. I'm sure of it."

"But you've never made this antidote before?" Diana stared at the boy incredulously.

"No, but it's okay! Really! I never made the mist of eternal sleep, either," the boy said. "And it worked quite remarkably, didn't it? The antidote will work. I'm sure it will."

"Undo the potion!" Diana shouted. "Fix it. Get whatever you need to make the antidote, mix it up, and wake them. Now!"

"I can't. The ingredients are back on my island. I'm sorry. I should have thought this through better. . . . I didn't have a lot of time. He gave me until daybreak before he destroys my land and everyone who lives there."

"All you had to do was tell me what the matter

was," Diana said. "I would have helped you. *We* would have helped you. This is an island of warrior women who never back away from the face of evil. And you've put them all to sleep!"

"I'm s-sorry. I shouldn't have done it. But I panicked. You haven't stared into his eyes like I have. The way he l-looks at you . . ." Augustus shuddered. "I didn't have a choice."

"And to save your people, you harmed mine," Diana said quietly.

Dark clouds began gathering in the distance. This was supposed to be the best week of the year. Diana should have been in her room eating sliced lemon cake and laughing with her best friend. Instead all the women on her island were enchanted and a nation beyond her shores was on the brink of being burned to the ground.

Diana swallowed. She'd never left Themyscira before in her life. The thought of leaving now, under these circumstances, and heading to a nation where a demon awaited her made her feel dizzy.

"And we can get to Sáz with the chariot you mentioned?" she finally asked.

"It's right there. Parked by the shoreline." He pointed to the beach. Gentle waves lapped the shore. The chariot was made of glass, open-backed with a wide platform to stand upon. It blended seamlessly into the background. It was no wonder they'd overlooked it.

"I know I don't deserve your help," he said. "You showed me kindness and generosity and I lied to you in return. I am so sorry."

The clouds in the distance rumbled. A shot of lightning burst through the night sky.

Diana would have given anything in the world to wake up the sleeping women to ask them what they should do. Her mother was a strategic thinker—she'd have come up with a plan in minutes. And Aunt Antiope's fighting skills were unrivaled. Together with the other Amazons, no person—or demon—would have stood a chance.

But none of the women on the island could help her now. If there was to be any hope of stopping this demon, saving Augustus's lands, and rousing Diana's own people from sleep, it was up to her.

Diana swallowed. Two communities—both her own and Augustus's—were counting on her. *Needed* her. And even though she wasn't a fully trained warrior, she needed to do whatever she could to save them.

"Fine," said Diana. She pushed down the worry churning inside of her. "I'll go with you."

"I'm coming, too," said Sakina. "Two heads are always better than one."

"It's dangerous." Diana hesitated. "And after what I accused you of, Sakina . . . I shouldn't have doubted you or your family. Not even for a second."

"He must have been a pretty good liar if you believed him."

"I *couldn't* believe it," Diana said. "But he seemed so sincere, and he was covered in bruises. . . . But I should have trusted my gut. I'm so sorry."

"We can sort this out later," Sakina replied. "I'm going with both of you and that's that."

"I d-don't know if all of us can go," Augustus said slowly. "The chariot's balance is fragile, and I brought only enough potion to calibrate it for two people."

"Mira can help pull the chariot, can't you, girl?" Sakina asked. The bird chirped excitedly and flew to the chariot.

"I'll take that as a yes," Diana said. "Could she help with the extra weight?"

"Might give it a little more oomph." Augustus nodded. "We can try."

The snow leopard mewled and tapped Sakina's feet with her paw.

"No, Arya." Sakina shook her head. "I know you want to protect us, but he said this thing can barely carry the three of us. Keep watch while we're gone? Make sure our mothers and the other women are safe?"

"We'll need the coordinates to return home," Diana said. "They're back at the palace."

"I still have mine on me." Sakina patted her belt.

"Th-there's also one more thing," Augustus said hesitantly, biting his lip.

"What's that?" asked Diana.

"I—I don't want to keep anything else from you. If you're going to help me, you should know the full extent of what you're getting into."

"We're listening," Diana said carefully.

"Before I left, he forced me to make a potion. He peppered it through the island."

"What kind of potion?" asked Sakina.

"It's a protection potion. It creates invisible force fields around whatever you want to keep safe. It also keeps anyone or anything from leaving."

"You mean to say if we go with you, we might never be able to leave? To return home?" Diana said slowly.

"I'm sorry," the boy said. His eyes brimmed with tears. "I tried to refuse. First I pretended I'd done it and made a fake potion; but when he tested it out and saw that it didn't work, he beat me." The boy waved at his bruises. "When he threatened to kill my father then and there, I buckled."

Diana studied Augustus. She still felt upset with him for deceiving her, but he'd been under enormous stress; that much was clear.

"Is there any way to undo the force field?" Diana asked. "Is there a potion to counter it?"

"Because I made the potion *for* the demon, the only one who can undo it is the demon." The boy trembled. "Unless he's destroyed. . . . If we can end him, the force field ends as well."

"So if we don't defeat the demon . . ." Sakina's voice trailed off.

"We won't ever return," Diana said. Her head spun with this new information. It was scary enough to leave Themyscira for the first time in her life and head for dangerous unknown terrain, but if they didn't defeat the demon, *they would never be able to come back home?* Diana turned toward the woods behind her. The windowed pillars of her palace home towered over the trees. Her head hurt. She wished there was another way. But they had to go, not only to destroy this demon but to get the antidote to wake up the enchanted women on Themyscira. Two nations depended on her. She had no idea if they could do it, but they had to try.

Tentatively, the three of them made their way to the shore. The wind blew furiously against Diana's body, as though trying to convince her to stay back. Close up, the chariot was larger than it had first seemed. Vines were etched into the edges of the glass. Augustus stepped on it and pulled a vial from his leather pouch. Upturning it over the chariot, the powder sprinkled out and was absorbed by the glass—and then the entire chariot began to shimmer and buzz. He dipped his fingers into the vial and drew out another pinch of powder, sprinkling it on Mira.

"Ready?" Diana asked Sakina.

"Not really," Sakina responded, eyeing the glass chariot. "But here we go."

Both girls stepped onto the chariot. And then, slowly, it began to rise.

"This is happening," said Sakina under her breath. "It's really happening."

Diana looked over the edge of the chariot as it rose into the sky. Her favorite olive tree shrank in the distance. The looming statue of Zeus atop a pillar on the south shore dwindled to the size of a matchstick. From this angle, the entire nation of Themyscira—her entire world until this moment—looked so small, she could encircle her fingers around all of it. She watched the island through the foggy mist of clouds until her homeland completely disappeared from view.

The moon shone to her left. Diana's heart fluttered. She had told Augustus she would help him, but now that they were leaving her home—flying thousands of feet above the ground—the full reality of the responsibility settled heavy inside her. The fate of two nations rested upon three kids.

We can do it, she told herself. *We can save his people. We can bring back the antidote to wake up the women.*

But could they really? Or was this a mission they couldn't possibly complete—or survive?

Chapter Seven

The night air brushed crisp and cool against Diana's skin as the chariot raced miles above the open sea toward Augustus's land.

"How far away are we?" Diana asked.

"Should be there soon," he said. "Hopefully."

"You doing okay, Mira?" Sakina asked the bird.

The bird chirped in reply, tugging the chariot's rope tighter with her beak. They'd been flying for ten minutes or so, and Sakina still gripped the edge of the chariot tightly. Her knuckles were white.

"Are you okay?" Diana asked her.

"I guess," Sakina said tersely. "Hoping I don't suddenly fall out of whatever this thing is."

"You won't," the boy replied. "Our chariots are very secure. I helped design this one myself."

"As if I'd believe anything you say," Sakina said.

His shoulders slumped. He didn't reply.

Diana glanced at Sakina.

"I wanted to say I'm sorry again," Diana said softly. "I should never have doubted you, even for a second."

"Yeah. You shouldn't have. But if you thought I really was doing something wrong, I guess I'm glad you called me out," Sakina said. "My mother always says we are supposed to enjoin the right and forbid the wrong. It's what you were trying to do. And anyway . . ."

Sakina's voice trailed off as the chariot suddenly lowered below a cluster of thick clouds—and there it was. A mass of land with lights glowing in the distance.

"That's my nation, Sáz," Augustus said. "We're almost there."

Diana looked at the island in wonder. It was smaller than she'd imagined, maybe half the size of Themyscira. With the moon shining through a patch of dark clouds, she could see how lush and green the island's center was, with forests of tropical palm trees reaching toward the sky. It was shaped like an enormous cylinder shooting straight out of the ocean.

"I've never seen anything like this," Diana said.

"It's a unique piece of land." Augustus nodded. "The gods fashioned it from an ancient volcano. The parts along the shoreline are flat and sandy with rocks and boulders along the edges and there's lots of trees leading uphill to the second plane, ringing the center there. The second plane is full of meadows and grassland. It's where I collect most of my plants for potion making."

"And the orange stream?" Sakina squinted at the island's center.

"It's a lava river," he said. "The lava is why no one lives on the second plane, even though it's really pretty. Our homes are atop the cliffs on the third plane, where you can see lights glimmering. The gods flattened it out to make it livable."

Diana looked at the river of lava, fiery and orange, spilling into the ocean from either side of the island and creating new earth. Had it been under better circumstances, Diana would have loved to wander and explore this strange and mystical land.

"Wait," Diana said. "Who are they?" As they flew closer, she could make out people standing motionless like statues on the top plane.

"My people," Augustus said quietly. "He's hypnotized every last one of them—they don't even sneeze unless he tells them to."

Diana looked at the stock-still people lining the land. A chill passed through her. Whatever he was, human or demon, he was a monster. They'd definitely need to muffle their ears once they landed so they, too, didn't get hypnotized.

Diana, Sakina, and Augustus continued flying, headed to the island's opposite side. As they approached, Diana spotted what seemed like a lit dock stretching out into the ocean. From where they flew, it looked like a line of glimmering silver. As they passed by, Diana could barely make out four men, tall and broad-shouldered, pacing its length. Another dock—this one unlit and empty—lay parallel to it in the distance.

"Are those your docks?" she asked.

"Yes. One of those structures—the brighter one—is more of a runway, though," he said. "The gods use it to take off and land with their chariots. The one next to it is our regular dock for boats and ships."

"And those men on the silver runway . . ." Sakina's voice trailed off.

"They're waiting for us," he said. "I told them I'd meet them there. But we're pretty high up and far away, so they won't see us land. I steered us at this precise angle to stay out of their line of sight or hearing."

Diana glanced at the boy. She still didn't know if she could trust him, but at least there was this. He hadn't turned them in immediately.

Suddenly she froze. The chariot was trembling. Until now it had flown smoothly without so much as a bump in the air.

"What's going on?" Diana asked. She gripped the edge against the sudden turbulence. Her body vibrated along with the vessel.

"Is the spell wearing off?" Sakina asked, glancing around.

"No way." Augustus shook his head. "I used enough powder for it to fly us three times as far. It can't be—"

The chariot sputtered before jerking forcefully to a stop in midair. Diana's head slammed into the glass edge. Skull throbbing, she peered over the side to see what they'd crashed into. But the tree line was hundreds of feet below them. Besides Mira pulling the chariot, there were no other birds or flying creatures of any sort in the night sky. *What is going on?* Diana turned to Augustus to ask, but before she could say a word, without warning, they plummeted.

Diana's heart leapt in her throat. Sakina crouched next to her, arms over her head, bracing for impact. The chariot dipped hundreds of feet, careening at full speed toward the ground. Augustus gritted his teeth and pulled at the reins. His face grew red from the effort. Instinctively Diana reached out to help him. She yanked on the ropes with him until the chariot screeched to a stop. They had pulled up in time to hover just above the treetops.

"What—is—happening?" Diana breathed out.

"I don't know!" Augustus shouted. "It's never done this before."

"We need to land it. Now!" Diana said.

"Yes, but—" Augustus's voice was drowned out by a sharp, splintering shriek.

Diana felt the blood leave her face.

This isn't happening! she thought frantically. *I'm dreaming. I must be.*

But it was no dream. Before her eyes, and still hundreds of feet above the ground, the front of the chariot began cracking in two.

"It's the protective potion at work! The force field!" Augustus shouted over the sound of breaking glass. "It's the only explanation!"

"You didn't plan for that?" Sakina yelled.

"I knew it stopped people from leaving. I didn't realize it could attack people coming in!"

"You have to land this. Now!" Diana yelled as the

chariot began shaking and plummeting again.

"I'm trying!" He strained against the reins as the chariot stopped and wobbled roughly from side to side. "It's not budging. We're stalled."

The crack along the front of the chariot grew wider. It split the front of the vessel in two and ripped along the glass floor beneath their feet like a zipper coming undone. Any minute now it would chop the chariot in half, leaving them to fall to their deaths.

"We need to jump!" Diana said. Her heart pounded in her ears. "It's our only shot."

"Jump where?" Sakina shouted. "We're too far up!"

"A tree?" Diana glanced below. "Maybe the branches could stop our fall?"

"Or knock us out." Sakina shook her head.

"Maybe," Diana said. "But we don't have a choice. I don't see where else we can go."

But before they could do anything, the chariot pitched forward and then dipped again, dropping dozens of feet until it slammed to a stop in midair.

Diana's stomach hurt. They'd moved farther away from the cluster of trees.

"To your left!" Augustus yelled. He pointed to a grassy stretch below them surrounded by a grove of trees. "If we jump right now from this angle, the odds are good we'll land on that soft patch of grass."

Diana hesitated. They were still quite far up. If they didn't fall exactly where Augustus pointed, they could break an arm or a leg . . . or worse.

An ear-splitting crunch filled the air. The front half of the glass chariot shattered and crumbled off; the debris fluttered like dust to the ground. A gaping space stared back from where the front of the chariot used to be.

Diana swallowed. They had to jump. There was no other choice.

"Let's go! Now!" she shouted.

"I can't!" Sakina's eyes watered. "We're going to get killed!"

"We'll definitely get killed if we let this thing break apart in the sky!" Diana reached over and squeezed Sakina's hand. "We have to jump. It's our only chance! One. Two. Three. Now!"

Diana's heart jammed into her throat as they leapt. Their bodies fell freely, spinning in the air. Mira's panicked chirps screeched in her ears. The dark scenery flashed by in a blur. Her stomach churned. Would this be the last memory she would ever have? Spiraling through the air to her death?

Within seconds she landed with a hard thump on dewy, damp grass. Diana lay still for a moment, stunned, and slowly pressed herself up by her elbows. She watched as the chariot nose-dived, shattering against a rocky outcrop by the shore. Her body ached from the fall, but looking at the pile of debris in the distance, she shuddered. It could have been much worse.

"That was close," Diana said softly. She rubbed her arms. They were bruised, but they would heal. Glancing around in the darkness, she squinted to make out the terrain. Light-colored rocks and tall boulders lined the shore's edge. The rest of the first plane—as Augustus had called it—was wooded, with lush green trees and a hill that stretched up behind them.

"Is everyone okay?" she asked.

"Think so," said Augustus. He sat across from her, gingerly inspecting his knee.

"Put me down as a solid *definitely not* okay," Sakina groaned.

Diana's eyes widened. Sakina hadn't been so lucky in her landing. She'd fallen a few steps farther from her and one of her legs seemed to have taken the brunt of the fall. Diana could see it was bent at an awkward angle and swelling fast.

"Don't move it!" Diana rushed to her friend's side.

"Couldn't move it if I wanted to," Sakina said through clenched teeth.

"Oh no." Augustus hurried over, pulling a jar from his leather pouch. "Looks like a break. I have a cream that can help. I'm accident-prone; I always keep it on me. Heals bones in a matter of seconds but stings a bit when you apply it."

"And how do I know your potion won't put me to sleep . . . or worse?" Sakina eyed the jar suspiciously.

"I—I don't blame you for not trusting me. Not sure I'd believe me either if I were you," Augustus said quietly. He pulled out the jar and dabbed some of the white cream on his own arm and then held it out for her. "The bones burn as they fuse back together and heal, but it won't harm you. I swear on my life."

"Fine." Sakina gritted her teeth. "Whatever makes this pain stop, I'll do it."

Her expression was pinched as he kneeled by her side and applied the cream.

"Give it a few seconds," he said. "It's fast-acting. But I can apply more if it doesn't take properly the first time."

They watched and waited. Sakina's expression grew flushed as she struggled against the pain. But then she exhaled. Before their eyes, the swelling began to go down.

"It worked." She stretched her leg out. Gingerly, she stood up and put her weight on it. She looked at Augustus. "That's incredible. . . . Thank you."

"Glad I can help," Augustus said. "It's the least I can do."

The clouds shifted, covering the moon's rays and enveloping the three of them in near-total darkness. Gone were all the visual markings. Even the trees were hidden beneath the blackness. The entire island looked like it had been dipped in ink.

"We should get a move on," Augustus said urgently. "If it stays this dark, it'll take us double the time to hike to the top plane."

"What's the best route?" Diana asked.

"There's only one direction to go," he said. "Up. But I think if we veer right, it's less likely to be muddy." He took a step back and pointed. "It also . . ."

The rest of his words died in his mouth.

His eyes grew wide. He tipped backward.

And suddenly he was gone.

Chapter Eight

At first Diana thought she'd imagined it. People didn't disappear into thin air.

Or did they?

"Augustus!" Diana called out. She scanned the darkened hillside and unfamiliar land.

"What happened?" Sakina said slowly.

A faint voice cried in the darkness.

"Down here! Help!"

"Augustus?" Diana glanced around. "Where are you?"

"Below you!"

She took a step forward and stopped with a start. The dirt beneath her feet crumbled, loose and soft.

"There's some kind of hole here," Diana whispered.

"Can you shine a light for us, Mira?" Sakina asked the bird.

Mira swooped down and settled on Sakina's shoulder. She blinked rapidly until her silver eyes lit beams into the darkness.

At the edge of Diana's feet lay a gaping pit. And there, at the bottom, was Augustus. He was coated in dirt. His eyeglasses were bent at an angle. He looked up at them with unmasked fear in his eyes.

Diana dropped to her knees and reached out her hands. The pit wasn't terribly deep, but it extended far enough that he'd need them to lend a hand if he was going to try to climb out.

"Can you grab my arm?" she asked him. "I'll have you up in no time."

"Can't . . . move . . . ," the boy whispered.

"Why not?" Diana asked. But then she gasped.

Spiders. Enormous ones. They teetered on spindly legs and looked like large, furry coconuts. There were at least forty of them. They swarmed the pit and surrounded Augustus.

"These—these are rapting spiders," Augustus said tensely. "A-any part of your body they bite gets infected and dies off. . . . There's no known antidote."

Three of the spiders lurched closer to Augustus. Diana's stomach turned.

"Can you talk to them?" Diana asked Sakina. "Tell them to stand back."

"I can try," Sakina said slowly.

She leaned down and clucked her tongue. She snapped her fingers. Looking down, she paused to listen. Then she clucked again and snapped louder.

"Well, I can talk to animals—but that doesn't mean they always listen to me." Sakina's expression was pale beneath Mira's silvery gaze.

"What did they say?" Diana asked.

"I told them to leave him alone. They said they were dropped here hours ago. A creature promised them they would receive a boy for a delicious meal so long as they left alone the girl he'd brought with him." She looked down at Augustus. "Is there anything else on the island that the spiders like to eat?"

"C-caribou," Augustus said. His voice shook with terror. The spiders stood close to him now, their legs brushing against his feet.

"Perfect." Sakina leaned down and spoke again. Diana watched tensely as the spiders hissed back at her. Sakina shook her head and bit her lip.

"What'd they say?" Diana asked.

"I told them there's a dead caribou over by the dock. They got excited but said the boy would make a fine appetizer before they went there."

"Let's pull you up. Now!" Diana insisted, extending her hand toward the boy.

"No!" Augustus shook his head quickly.

"I know it's risky. But it's better than being eaten alive!"

"They bite with lightning speed. If they get any idea I'm even thinking about it, it'll be over."

Diana watched more spiders creep closer and closer to Augustus. She'd never known spiders could grow so big. Or look this sinister. Themyscira didn't have vicious creatures like this. She wondered what other horrors lay in wait for them on this new, strange island.

Mira perched on Sakina's shoulder. Suddenly Diana jolted.

"Sakina!" Diana exclaimed. "Can you tell them that if they don't get to the caribou now, Mira will beat them to it?"

"You think they'll buy it?" Sakina eyed the bird. "She's kind of, um . . . small."

"She might be tiny," Diana said. "But what about her whole crew of birds flying fast toward the island? Together they can eat the caribou in a matter of seconds."

Sakina smiled. "A trick within a trick. I like it."

Sakina spoke again. Urgently, she pointed to the bird. The spiders clicked and snapped.

Diana held her breath. Would it work?

Abruptly, the spiders turned from Augustus. Forming a line, they clicked their jaws and climbed up the other side of the pit. Then, one by one, they disappeared into the night.

Diana's body felt weak with relief. It worked.

"Hurry!" Augustus called out. "They'll be back, and when they are, they'll be angry."

Both girls held their hands out. He grasped their

palms, and then, his feet digging into the dirt walls, he made his way up and out of the shallow pit.

Stumbling onto the grass, he bent at the waist and gasped. His body trembled.

“I thought I was d-done for,” he said shakily. “You both saved my life. Thank you.”

They started heading toward the nearby tree line. “Why would someone dig this up in the middle of nowhere?” Diana asked.

“It’s new,” Augustus said. “I know every inch of this land. There’s no way it was here before tonight.”

“Fits what the spiders said about being dropped here just hours earlier,” Sakina told them.

“We’ll need to be careful,” Diana began as they entered the cover of trees. “There could be more of them and—” She startled. Just ahead, over Sakina’s shoulder, a thick net of rope sewn into a spiderweb-like design swung toward them like a catapult. “Duck!” she shouted.

Instantly, they dropped flat to the ground. The air swooshed above them, the contraption missing them by a hairsbreadth.

The three of them stared at the net, swinging loose in the air behind them.

"And that was not there before, either," the boy said flatly.

Sakina gasped. "Is that a spiderweb from the spiders we just tricked?"

"Rapting spiders don't weave webs of rope." Augustus shook his head.

"Traps," Diana said slowly. "The demon set out traps."

"He didn't do it himself," Augustus said. "The knotting on it—those are triple knots—the same as the ones we use on our specialty chariots. He enchanted my people to do his dirty work while I was gone."

"How many traps could he have laid out for us?" Sakina asked, glancing around.

"I haven't been gone all that long," said Augustus. "It can't be all that many. . . ."

His voice trailed off because just then the clouds parted slightly. Enough for the moon to reveal the island stretching into the distance before them. Looking around, Diana gasped.

"Are those . . . bear traps?" Sakina asked, her voice a whisper. She pointed to a metal claw partially buried beneath the dirt just steps away.

"Not only bear traps," Augustus said softly, gesturing to the hillside.

Panic flooded through Diana as she followed his gaze. Some of the traps were covered haphazardly with fallen leaves and branches, but it was impossible to miss most of them: Freshly turned earth, betraying more pits. Nets tied to trees. Metal teeth opened wide and scarcely hidden. As far as they could see—the entire perimeter of the island leading to the second plane was filled with traps.

For *her.*

Chapter Nine

Silently, they took in the hillside before them. Two tightly coiled nets lay fastened to the ground near their feet. Metallic edges of other entrapments and contraptions stretched across the rocky, tree-lined mountainside.

"There are hundreds of them," Diana said slowly. "They're everywhere."

"He must have had everyone on the island working on it while I was away," said Augustus. "There's too many of them laid out. There's no other logical explanation."

It was hard for Diana to wrap her mind around how one person managed to control so many people simply with what he said and how he said it. Her lasso could reveal the truth, but it didn't compel people to commit heinous acts against their will. The demon had a power more dangerous than any sword or weapon.

"We'll have to be extra careful," Sakina said. "I can offer to be— Whoa!"

She leapt back.

"My foot started sliding!" she exclaimed. "Is that . . . Is it a rope . . . with *blades*?"

Looking at the ground, they saw that, indeed, a rope lined with sharp spikes lay tucked among pine needles mere steps from where they stood.

"Another trap," Augustus said, grim.

"He's creative," Sakina grumbled. "Should've used his talents to take up painting or something useful."

Diana looked at the metal teeth. Her stomach hurt. Sakina broke her leg falling from the chariot. Augustus was almost devoured by spiders. Danger lurked everywhere they turned. The demon remained a mystery to her, but the only known constant was that he had done everything in his power to get to her.

"Don't be so worried. He's definitely dangerous,

but we've got this." Sakina put an arm around Diana's shoulder. "We'll outsmart him. Just have to figure out what makes him tick."

"Not 'we.' Me," Diana said.

"Excuse me?" Sakina asked.

"Augustus, if you can talk me through the rest of the path and where I need to go, I can take it from here."

"You're kidding, right?" Sakina asked. "This is literally the worst possible timing for a joke."

"It's me he wants. Why should you both put yourselves in harm's way?"

"I can understand your line of thinking." Augustus adjusted his glasses. "But I know this island better than both of you. The demon will be up on the third plane, at the very top. It's flat and smooth up there—but it is definitely *not* simple getting there. You have to know your way around or you'll wind up walking in circles. And"—he cleared his throat—"I'm the reason you're here. I have to help you."

"And I'm not a snow leopard you can just order to hang back," Sakina retorted.

"No. You're my *best friend.*" Diana's voice cracked.

"You could have died when the chariot broke apart."

"Okay. How about this? I'll hang back and let you go on your own." Sakina folded her arms. "But only if you can answer this question: If I was being targeted by a vapor demon, would you sit back, wish me luck, and watch me go on my way?"

"Come on," Diana protested. "That's different."

"It's exactly the same," she replied with pursed lips. "And you know it."

Diana smiled a little. This much was true. She'd never allow anyone—let alone her best friend—to face known danger without being there to help.

"Fine," Diana said. "Let's destroy the demon together. But before we do, we have to figure out how we're getting to the next plane of the island without getting caught in one of these traps."

"Mira can help us out," said Sakina.

The bird fluttered over to them.

"Can you fly overhead and see where the traps are?" Sakina asked the creature. "Maybe with your bird's-eye view you can find us a path to safely follow."

Mira chirped and flew into the night. Beams of

light shot like sparks on the ground all around them. Returning after a few minutes, she swept down to pull on Sakina's sleeve with her beak and chirped.

"Mira says the safest way forward is on the left. There's still some danger, but she said it's the best bet," Sakina said. "She'll light the way."

The three of them scrambled up the hillside, following a worn path with the bird leading the way. Ancient trees and twisting branches grew on either side. Diana's calves already ached from the vertical ascent. Augustus wasn't joking when he said this part of Sáz was steep.

"Whoa!" Augustus burst out.

"What's the matter?" Diana asked.

"I tripped over something." He bent down to examine the dirt. "Is that . . . a wire?"

A sharp whistling noise sounded through the trees.

"Step back!" Diana yanked Augustus away as an arrow flew past them, slamming into a tree to their left.

The three of them stared at the metal arrow. It was wedged halfway into the trunk.

"That was . . . c-close." Sakina's voice shook.

"Looks like it was fashioned out of our specialty carving tools," Augustus said. His voice trembled. "The ones w-we use to add d-details, like leaves and flowers, to the chariots. They've been weaponized."

"He wants to kill me," Diana said slowly.

"No." Augustus shook his head. "He was clear he needed you alive. These arrows are positioned low; they'd incapacitate you, but they wouldn't kill you."

"Well, *that*'s reassuring," Sakina muttered.

Kneeling, Diana saw thin wires pressed against the ground, tightly wound and stretching toward distant trees, where metal makeshift arrows poised against a line of trunks, ready to deploy in their direction at the slightest touch. The wires were only inches from one another.

"They stretch to the white boulder up ahead." Diana squinted. "It's a good twenty feet away. . . ."

"We can divert through the trees on either side of the path to avoid them," said Sakina.

"But what if there's worse waiting for us in the forest? Mira led us this way for a reason. We can do this. But we have to take our time and focus," Diana said. She hoped she sounded more confident than she felt.

Gingerly, the three of them stood on their tiptoes. One by one, with Diana in the lead, they stepped over the next wire—careful to not so much as graze it. She tried her best to push out the image of the arrows pressed against the tree trunks, waiting for the smallest misstep to deploy.

"Three more to go . . . ," Sakina murmured as they continued to tread.

"Two now," Augustus said hopefully, after they successfully avoided another trip wire.

"And one!" Diana said, jumping onto the white boulder beyond the treacherous section of traps.

Diana exhaled with relief as Augustus and Sakina clambered onto the rock.

"Before we continue, we just have to do one thing." Diana leaned down and gathered pebbles from the ground. With a flick of her wrist, she skipped them along the wires.

Within seconds metal arrows sliced through the air across from where they stood.

"What are you doing?" Augustus asked.

"She's making sure they don't deploy on anyone else," Sakina said.

"Exactly." Diana nodded. "Can't undo all these traps, but we have to at least try disarming the most dangerous ones. No one should have to risk getting sliced with an arrow."

They continued uphill with Mira guiding the way. The farther they walked, the more strenuous the uphill hike grew. Part of Diana felt tempted to scamper up the hill as fast as she could, to put the grueling hike behind her, but it wasn't worth the risk. There was no telling what danger awaited them—one small misstep could spell the end.

They skirted around deep pits that popped up on either side of them, yawning wide into the darkness. They hopped over steel blades sticking straight out of the earth, awaiting an unsuspecting foot.

"Stay low," Diana warned. They approached a tree whose low-hanging branches stretched above their path. "Not sure anything's up there, but you never know."

Inching closer, she peered through the leaves. A brown rope dangled amidst the branches. Looking at the ground, Diana pointed at the trip wire snaking through the dirt.

"He's determined," Sakina grimly said as they stepped over it. "Gotta give him that much."

"How much longer until we're on the second plane?" Diana asked, glancing at the darkness ahead of them. It would have been hard enough for one person to evade all the traps they'd encountered, but three people? Her stomach hurt from worry about what more might lie ahead.

"Shouldn't be long," Augustus said. "We're going so slow, it's taking longer than it normally would."

Augustus's breathing grew heavy the farther they journeyed. She saw him clutch his arm, wincing from pain. His elbow hadn't fully healed yet. Diana's own calves ached. Sakina's forehead trickled with perspiration. But they didn't stop moving. They kept climbing until at last the steep uphill ascent gave way to a flat, flower-filled meadow. A rush of relief passed through Diana.

"We made it," Sakina said. She collapsed onto the grass and wiped her brow.

Diana looked around. Even under the darkness of night, the second plane was undeniably beautiful. Trees flanked with colorful leaves—red, pink, and yellow—and flowering bushes lined the edges of a towering granite cliff. Wildflowers filled the grassy meadow. A sulfuric smell from the river of lava they'd seen overhead wafted to them now. Diana pinched her nose. But even the odor wasn't enough to erase the beauty.

"This is incredible," Diana said. "Almost hard to believe it's real."

"I wish you could see it all in the daylight," Augustus said. "When Mr. Broderick is too busy with customers, I come down here and check out new herbs and plants for myself. It's my personal potion-making playground. I was here when the demon arrived."

"Are we close to the top now?" Diana asked. "Where the demon is?"

"If he's still where he was when I left, we're about halfway there."

Only halfway? Diana sighed.

"There are cliffs all around us here, but I'll lead us to the path that will take us straight up."

"Can you tell us anything more about him?" Sakina asked. They walked toward the uphill path with their sides pressed against the smooth cliff wall, shrouded by trees. "The hypnotism sounds familiar. Anything, even small details, might jog my memory."

"He arrived early in the morning, in a rowboat. At least, I assume so. There's an unfamiliar wooden one anchored on the dock's edge. It's not one of ours."

"No one questioned why a random person showed up to your island?" Sakina asked.

"I don't think anyone would have thought he was up to anything nefarious," Augustus replied. "The gods protect us. We don't even have an army. Who needs one when Zeus has your back? By the time my people saw he wasn't walking but floating, it was probably too late; he'd hypnotized them with his voice."

"This demon's got a death wish if he's trying to

mess with a place the gods protect," Sakina said.

"That's what I can't stop thinking about." Augustus shook his head. "I tried to come up with different hypotheses for what is going on, but none of them make sense. And if he can get around the gods, how can *we* stop him?"

"I guess the first thing is to make sure *we* don't get enchanted," Diana said.

"Right." He stopped. "I almost forgot."

Augustus kneeled down and plucked two fuzzy flowers from the ground. They were all different colors and scattered throughout the meadow.

"I used these petals." He handed them to the girls. "You'll still be able to hear, but it muffles the noise a bit."

Both girls crumpled the petals and stuffed them into their ears.

"Wow! It tickles." Sakina giggled.

It was true. Diana laughed a little. The flower felt soft and fuzzy in her ears, but if it did the job of protecting them from being hypnotized, it was perfect. Suddenly she straightened.

"Did you feel that?" she asked.

"No." Sakina shook her head. "I didn't—"

Diana pressed a finger to her lips. The vibration grew louder.

"Footsteps," Sakina whispered.

"It's my people." Augustus paled. "The demon probably sent them. They're coming. For us."

Chapter Ten

The vibrations beneath them grew louder. They were close. The three of them would be found out any second. They needed to do something—*now*.

"We have to hide," Diana said breathlessly. "What's the safest place? Any caves in these cliffs? A structure of any kind to slip into?"

Augustus scanned the forest. Then he nodded.

"Follow me," he whispered.

The trio hurried in the opposite direction, taking care to stay shrouded behind the trees lining the granite cliff to their left. The footsteps grew louder.

Diana thought about her sword tucked into her belt. She'd never used it to fight anyone in *actual* combat. Now Diana wondered: If it came down to it, could she do it? Could she fight to save herself and her friends?

"There!" Augustus said. He raced to a thick sequoia tree and peered inside. Within seconds, he disappeared.

Sakina and Diana followed suit. The hollowed-out tree was cool and dark inside. They peered out through a narrow opening, small as a keyhole. Seconds later, men appeared and raced past the tree.

Diana felt weak with relief. They'd almost been caught. But they'd hid just in time.

Diana counted them: twenty men in total. They held thick clubs. Some had white-blond hair, others a sandy brown. They looked like older versions of Augustus. But their expressions were blank. Their buttoned shirts fluttered against the breeze with each step. Were it not for the dead look in their eyes, they would seem like regular people on their way to an important errand. Wordlessly they stalked past the kids and off into the distance.

After a minute or so, Sakina whispered, "Is it clear?"

"Augustus said there's only one path up, so they'll be back," said Diana. "He's probably got them on patrol duty to look for us. Let's make sure they're safely gone before we step out and try to use the path."

Sure enough, a few moments later footsteps sounded again. The men rounded a corner and stomped past them, and then their footsteps faded away.

"That was close," Sakina said.

"Too close," Diana said. "How long do you think we have before they come back, Augustus?"

Augustus didn't respond. When she looked at him, his face was as white as mist, his expression haunted.

"Augustus, are you all right?" she asked gently.

"I know they're hypnotized," he said in a shaky voice. "But it's hard to see them like that. Ferdinand and his brothers—they run the corner bakery. Make the freshest biscuits you could imagine; soft on the inside and crispy on the outside. And Silvio—he was in the back—he's cut my hair since I was up to his knee. They're good people. There's a ninety-nine point nine percent probability that not one of those people hunting for us would hurt so much as a fly. But now they have clubs. And their eyes . . . It's scary to see them so blank. Like the lights are off and no one is home."

"This must be so hard to see. But it's not them. Not really," Diana said. "He's hijacked their minds."

"You're right," he said. "But I don't know why . . . it still hurts."

Diana looked at his crushed expression. If any of the women of her island—Cylinda and Yen, or Aunt Antiope—were hunting for *her,* even if she could explain away *why,* she would have been devastated, too.

"We'll fix this," Diana reassured him. "We'll do everything we can. But we need to act fast. Who knows when they'll be back."

With the petals still blocking their ears and muffling the noise around them, Diana kept her eyes peeled, glancing about with each step they took.

"I could get the Lasso of Truth around him," said Diana as they hurried along, still wary of hidden traps. "I'd have to figure out *how,* but once the demon's caught, he'll confess. They believe everything he says, so when he tells them the truth, they'll believe that, too, won't they?"

"But the demon is made of vapor," Augustus said. "Can the lasso work on him?"

"I'm not sure." Diana's confidence wavered.

"Could you tell us more about what the demon was like?" Sakina asked. "Any funny characteristics? What exactly did his voice sound like?"

"He spoke with a growl. Like the voice was scraping against his throat to get out. He wore a black robe," Augustus said. "It had an orange stripe down the back."

"Orange stripe," Sakina said, frowning. "Was he tall?"

"Yes. He stood a foot taller than the tallest person on our island. And he was skinny, too. Like a pole."

A cackle burst through the air then. It was faint, in the distance, but the sound was impossible to miss. High-pitched and intense. Though their ears were muffled, the sound pulsed through the air and ricocheted against their skin like drops of rain.

"That's him," Augustus whispered. His eyes looked haunted.

"That laugh . . . ," Sakina said slowly. "He's a Bulnama demon. I read that they cackle at a high-pitched volume in pulsing beats. I read about him last week! The Bulnama demons stand out because they're rare. There's only a handful of them in the world. They have a solid orblike thing floating in the middle of them that keeps them ticking. And they're obsessive. Bounty hunters by trade. They've destroyed entire nations trying to search for one small item." She sighed. "I wish I could remember how to destroy them."

"If the orb is solid, that's it, then," Augustus said, and a small smile formed on his face. "If I can come up with something to destroy the *orb,* it'll probably be enough to destroy all of him."

"You think?" Diana asked hopefully.

"I'm not positive," he said slowly. "But if I can get the right ingredients together—ones that disrupt ions with full intensity, along with an acidic kicker to break it all down . . . and if we can mix it all in the proper order, we *might* be able to dispel him."

"What sorts of ingredients do you think you need?" Diana asked. She'd have far preferred a surefire way to destroy the demon, but this was the first hopeful thing she'd heard since they arrived.

"Water to help mix it up would be first." Augustus tapped his foot. "Running water is the purest, so that would be ideal. Oh! And slington berries. They grow up against the cliff walls. We use them on the island as a cooling agent for everything from fevers to stray lava burns. But the other two things we'll need . . ." His expression grew clouded. "Those will be trickier."

"How come?" Diana asked, studying his worried expression.

"The icta seed we need for the one-two punch of acidity to disrupt his properties are in a flower in a wooded patch of forest near the town center. Getting *into* the forest without being spotted might be tricky. The last time I was here, my people were lying in wait, zombified, not far from the pathway. And then there's the matter of the flume, the other ingredient. It's probably the most important one but also the most dangerous to procure."

"But you have it on the island?" Diana said.

"We have *one*—at least, we did the last time I checked. It's not far from here," he said somberly. "It's a mushroom. It's the most acidic living fungus in the world. I've only ever seen it once, when I was having a lesson with Mr. Broderick. Getting it is tricky and mixing it will be trickier because we have to do it at the very last minute. It loses power rapidly once it meets other chemical properties."

"But if we manage to get all the ingredients," Diana asked, "can we destroy him?"

"I think so," he said. "If we get the timing exactly right, there's no logical reason why it couldn't work. The mushroom alone has felled far greater foes in human history."

"Sublime!" said Sakina. She pumped her fists. "Lead the way."

Diana bit her lip. She wanted to be as excited as Sakina, but even if Augustus had high hopes for their experiment, it was still an experiment. And it was one that could not fail. Not only did their lives depend on it, but so did the lives of two nations.

"The flume grows beneath a bush across from the lava river. It's fragile, so it stays tucked under other plant life to keep from disintegrating in the heat."

"Is there a way over the river?" Sakina asked.

"There's a rope bridge, but the situation is more complicated. Lava doesn't flow like a river of water. Hot magma spews and splashes up from time to time. If it hits you, you could suffer severe burns and even die."

"So we'll just have to be careful," Diana said. She tried to keep a brave face. Lingering near a river of fire was the exact opposite of what she'd rather do, and Augustus's worried expression didn't make her feel confident, but if they had to extract the flume to destroy the demon, then there was no time for fear to take root.

The trio reversed course and headed toward the other side of the meadow. They moved silently, keeping a petal-filled ear out for the sounds of more guards. Passing a thick grove of banyan trees, they walked toward a waterfall, the water gliding gently down a cliff and splashing into a clear pond below. Augustus edged up to the flowing water and filled his canteen. He closed the lid and glanced up. His expression fell.

"The berries are up there." He pointed above their heads. "Higher than I anticipated."

A red plant jutted out of the cliffside twenty feet above them.

"There's no way for us to climb it, but maybe Mira can grab it for us?" Diana asked.

"She sure can," Sakina said.

The bird fluttered to the plant. With her beak, she carefully plucked a branch of berries and flew down, depositing it in Sakina's hand.

"Thanks, Mira." Augustus placed a few berries in the canteen and shook it.

"Well, that seemed easy enough!" Sakina said with apparent relief.

"Yes. We just have the mushroom and icta seed left," Diana agreed. They'd crossed off half their list in a matter of moments. After all they went through scaling the first plane of Sáz and hiding from the men with clubs, at least this part seemed simple. "Which way to the flume?"

"Well." Augustus hesitated. "The next part is . . . trickier," he said. "It's just . . . well, you'll see."

Sakina and Diana followed Augustus around the bend. He stopped.

"There it is." He lifted his finger and pointed.

Following his gesture, Diana froze.

"Holy moly," Sakina whispered.

The river of lava. It lay fifty steps away from them, down a clifflike bank, perhaps twenty feet below where they currently stood. From overhead, the orange glow of the lava stream had looked impressive—but now, as they approached it, the river was terrifying. Steam rose from the embankments. Stepping closer to observe the river from above, they watched a reedy branch fall from a nearby tree and into the lava. It caught fire and burned, vanishing in seconds. A narrow wooden bridge tied together with rope swung over the river, leading to a square patch of green, where a flowering bush pressed against a towering granite cliff.

"Looks a little flimsy," Diana said carefully. The bridge trembled and swayed from the force of the lava flowing below.

"A little?" Sakina raised an eyebrow. "It looks like a barbecue grill."

"It's . . . it's not the safest," Augustus said carefully. "We've had to replace it more times than I can count. And getting the mushroom is a three-person job: two of us to part the bush and one to carefully extract it, making sure not to touch it directly in any way and not to crush it between your fingers."

"Luckily there's three of us," Diana said.

"Yes, but the square patch of grass is small," Augustus said nervously. "I've never actually crossed the bridge without an adult before."

"We'll make it work," Diana said. "We have to."

The closer they approached, the louder the river of lava roared and hissed. Angry bubbles burst along the edges of the riverbank. Tentatively, she took a step onto the bridge. The wooden planks trembled violently beneath her feet. The sharp stench from the river made her eyes water. She clutched the thin, taut ropes on either side and took one careful step forward. Then another. The middle of the bridge sagged low. Glancing down, she saw orange fire flowing an arm's length below her; the heat of the lava lingered inches from her feet. Tightening her grip, she kept her eyes fixed on the patch of land on the other side until at last she felt the cool relief of grass beneath her feet. Augustus followed next. He tiptoed, careful to not let his feet linger over the wide gaps between the planks; his cheeks flushed pink from the heat when he finally reached her.

"Last but not least," Sakina announced. "I think I'll be the one to—"

Her eyes widened as she pitched forward, her boot caught in the gap between two planks.

"Sakina! No!" Diana cried out.

Sakina tried catching her balance but stumbled. The gaps between each step of the bridge were wide—wide enough for her to fall through entirely, if her leg shifted to just the right angle. Diana rushed toward her as she teetered precariously, but Sakina grabbed the edge of the bridge just in time to steady herself. Carefully, straining, she stood up and pulled her foot out of the gap. With both hands grasping the rope railing on either side of the bridge, Sakina carefully walked over to join the others.

"What *was* that?" Diana murmured. Then she saw: Sakina had tripped over a loose board. A rope connecting the planks had come undone.

"That was close," Sakina said shakily once she hopped onto the shore. "Thought I was about to actually get cooked."

Diana watched the rope tensely. It had slipped from where it had lain on the bridge and now swung inches from the bubbling lava below. Goose bumps trailed her arms. They needed to act fast.

"Where can we safely store the mushroom once we get it?" Diana asked.

"I have space in my bag." Augustus opened a small compartment. "Sakina, maybe you can help me part the bush, and then Diana can carefully remove the flume and place it inside this pocket."

Carefully, Sakina and Augustus parted the bush. Diana scanned the ground. The flume was tucked in the center—cream-colored, the size of a marble.

"Take your time. It looks harmless, but it's one of the most dangerous living organisms in the world," Augustus said. "Make sure it doesn't touch any part of your body. It'll burn straight through flesh."

Diana pulled a thick green leaf from the bush. Using it like a napkin, she gingerly pulled out the mushroom. It released from the ground with a gentle popping sound. Drawing it out of the bush, she marveled at how it looked—speckled red and white. It looked smooth as an egg.

"Perfect." Augustus opened his pocket as wide as he could. "Don't let it brush against the edge. There you go," he said as Diana delicately placed it inside. He buttoned it closed.

"Great!" said Sakina. "One last ingredient to go now. We should have a good strategy for slipping into the woods once we're up at the top plane."

"We can discuss that after we've crossed the bridge," Diana said quickly. "There's no telling—"

"No—" Augustus gasped.

The rope from the plank Sakina had tripped on dangled dangerously close to the lava below. It flickered above the orange river, moments from catching fire.

"We have to go! Now!" Diana said.

But before any of them could take a step, the rope grazed the river below. In seconds, red flames spiraled up the rope. The three of them watched, horror-struck, as the entire bridge was quickly consumed in an angry blaze. The fire roared, growing ten feet above them, the intense heat fanning against their faces. Plank by plank, each step of the bridge crumbled to ash, until the entire structure disappeared, enveloped by the orange lava below.

They stared in silence at the gaping river before them.

"This can't be happening," Sakina said with a trembling voice. She pressed her back against the smooth granite cliff behind her.

"There has to be another way across," Diana said.

"It's . . . it's impossible," Augustus said. "There's no way across a river this wide."

"Well, if we can't cross it, at least no one else can, either," Sakina said.

"The demon is made of vapor," Diana said. "He

doesn't need to walk. He can float over to us. And we don't have all the ingredients we need to destroy him."

"So it's over," Augustus said quietly.

No, Diana wanted to say. *It's not over. We still have a chance. We'll figure a way out of this.*

But once she glanced at the river—the granite cliff stretching hundreds of feet above them to the third plane—her words of encouragement faded on her tongue.

Because Augustus was right.

There was no way out.

So it was over?

Had the demon truly won?

Chapter Eleven

They stared at the gaping river of fire before them. Mira fluttered over and perched on Sakina's shoulder.

Diana's chest hurt. This couldn't be over. They had to do something.

But what? They were trapped. If they couldn't find a way to get over the lava river, they couldn't save Themyscira and Sáz. There was no guarantee they would even make it out alive.

"Now's the time to say 'I told you so,'" Sakina said with a wavering voice.

"What are you talking about?" Diana asked.

"This is all my fault," Sakina said. Her eyes brimmed with tears. Her maroon tunic was battered by their journey; the bottom of it was dusty and ripped along the edge. "I can't believe my clumsiness started the fire. I should've stayed back, like you said."

"It's my fault," Augustus said. "I'm the one who brought you both here. This was an impossible mission from the start."

"This is *not* either of your fault," Diana told them firmly. "We've been a great team. We wouldn't even have known for sure this was a demon in the first place without you," Diana told Sakina. "And Augustus is making the potion to destroy him. We won't give up. We *can't.*"

"I don't see a way out of it," Sakina said.

"Me either," said Augustus. "There's no way to cross the river."

"Maybe we shouldn't look at the river." Diana studied the cliff. "Maybe we try to scale this thing. Is there any way to get up to the next plane from here?"

"You'd have as good a chance at flying over it than climbing it without a vine or rope," Augustus said. "We rappel down the cliffsides here with vines sometimes, but even with a vine it's tricky to get *up.* The cliff is too smooth."

Diana examined the stone wall. It was brighter in color than the ones back in Themyscira—taller by at least a hundred feet, too—and it looked smooth as a sheet of paper.

"There's got to be some grooves in the stone," Diana murmured, brushing her hands against the granite. She peered at the trees lining the edge of the cliff. "What's up there at the top? Looks like a forest."

"It's the patch of woods where the icta seed is located. It's just off the town center where we saw the hypnotized people lined up in rows. . . . The demon is probably still there, too."

"We have to get up there," said Diana. "This cliff is the only way."

"I read a book about a man who scales cliffs with his bare hands," Sakina said. "Doesn't even need ropes. He said if you can find your footing, even in the smallest of spots, you can go farther than you think." She pressed her palms against the cliff and craned her neck upward. "See the bump over here?"

She trailed her hand along the granite. "Maybe I can climb a bit and see what else lies ahead."

Grunting, Sakina pressed down and tried to lift herself up, but her boot slipped. Her arms scraped against the rough rock wall as she skidded back down to the ground.

"Ow." She rubbed her elbow. "I guess you can't solve *everything* by reading."

Just then Augustus froze, his green eyes wide. "How long has it been since we saw the patrol?" he asked.

"Not sure," Sakina answered. "Thirty or forty minutes, maybe?"

"If they're circling the island, it won't take long for them to get back here." Augustus chewed his lip. "They'll find us here in about twenty minutes."

Diana looked at the stream of hot lava, thinking. "And even though they won't be able to cross the river . . ."

"Once they see us trapped here, they'll tell the demon," Augustus finished for her.

"And then we're done," Sakina said softly.

"No. There *has* to be a way," Diana said.

"I've lived here my whole life," Augustus said. "It's impossible to get up that cliffside without help."

But nothing is impossible, is it? Diana thought. There was always hope if you knew where to look for it.

She spread her palms against the granite and traced the rock carefully with her fingers. Palm to palm, the grainy texture of this wall was similar to her beloved olive tree back home. Diana knew how to firmly grip the practically invisible grooves along the trunk to shimmy her way to the branches above. The tree was not as tall or as wide as this granite monolith, but maybe Diana could scale it if she channeled the olive tree. Just maybe she could do it.

"Diana," Sakina warned. "Don't even think about it. It's too dangerous."

"It feels like my favorite tree back home." Diana gestured to the cliff.

"Seriously? You can't compare this cliff to a skinny little olive tree! If you lose your footing half-way up . . ." Sakina's voice trailed off.

"But what other options do we have?" asked

Diana. "I won't stay here and wait for them to catch us. We have to try. This is our only shot."

She put her hands on her hips and studied the cliff.

"See that little bump up there?" Diana pointed to a ledge of rock the size of a fingernail, just out of her reach. It was a few inches above the one Sakina had tried to grab. "If I can get ahold of the one Sakina reached for first and then jump and grab ahold of that next one, I can press my feet into the tiny little ridge after it, and from there I can figure out another groove to grip next. I just need a boost to get me to the first one."

"Diana, gravity can't be compromised," Augustus said carefully. "If you try to climb up and even miss one small groove . . . and if they hear you . . . the demon won't be far from the edge of the cliff."

"Augustus is right," said Sakina. "It's a humongous risk; you could fall to your death. We can't take that kind of chance."

"We don't have time for another strategy," Diana said urgently. "Let me try this. Help boost me up."

She inhaled and exhaled deeply and tried her best to still her mind. The cliff loomed high above them, and this task would require complete concentration. There was no room for hesitation or second-guessing.

Sakina shot her a worried look, but both she and Augustus reluctantly laced their hands together and kneeled by the wall. Diana gingerly placed a foot on their palms, then stood. They lifted her—and then she jumped.

The tips of her fingers gripped the tiny jagged edge pushing out from the wall. Clenching it with all her strength, she pulled herself up and scanned for another hold. Her face flushed. It wasn't easy to support her entire body with her fingertips. Mira fluttered over then and lit the wall with her gaze.

"Thanks, girl," Diana said with relief.

Scanning the wall, she found the next ledge. It was harder to reach than it had looked from the ground. Contorting her body, Diana placed the toe of one boot onto the ledge and tested her weight until she felt secure, and then she looked up to find something else to grab. The next tiny ledge was higher; Diana stretched her arms as far as she could, but before she could hook her fingers, her hand slipped. Her body slid down. Her knees scraped against the unforgiving rock. She shot a foot out to catch herself and exhaled when she found a toehold. Steadying herself, Diana closed her eyes. *Breathe,* she reminded herself. Another wrong move would send her tumbling to her death.

Carefully, bit by bit, skimming the cliff with her palms, she found the smallest of grooves and dug her fingertips or the toes of her boots as deep as she could, slowly making her way up.

Her body ached with every passing minute. Sweat dripped down her forehead. The vertical summit of the first plane had felt painful, but it paled in comparison to this. Diana didn't dare peek down, but looking up, she shivered—it was almost as scary.

And then she hit a roadblock.

Diana grew still. Worry snaked across her mind. Until now she'd managed to find something, no matter how small, to prop herself up and keep on climbing. The rock before her, though, showed no more ridges or ledges to hold—at least not as far as she could see.

Diana held on tight and looked around frantically. Mira flashed her eyes to help her search—but there was nothing to grip; the cliff here was as smooth as marble. Diana's feet strained against the small outcrop beneath her toes. With each passing second, her arms grew heavier and heavier as she tried to balance on practically nothing.

Diana stretched her body and reached as far as she could, hoping desperately for something to grasp. It was too late to try and get back down to Augustus and Sakina—she was very high up now. She needed to jump, to literally take a leap of faith and see if she could grab something above. Diana's heart hammered in her chest. *Here goes nothing,* she thought. Gritting her teeth, she fanned out her fingers and leapt.

Her fingertips brushed against something—or, rather, they slipped into nothing. There was a gap in the flat rock above her, a fracture so thin that it was impossible to see from her current position. Relief coursed through her body. Gripping the fine edge with one hand, she pulled herself up. It was a narrow crack straight through the rock. It tore up the cliffside, seemingly to the top. At least, Diana hoped it did.

Diana painstakingly worked her way up until she could securely wedge one foot and grip the upper edges of the gap with her palms. Gritting her teeth, she scooted her body up inch by inch toward the top edge of the cliff. Drenched in sweat, she finally reached up a hand and felt the welcoming touch of grass beneath her fingers.

She'd made it.

Diana wiggled herself over the edge and rolled onto the safety of the ground.

I did it, Diana thought. She caught her breath and peeked at Augustus and Sakina below. From this vantage point, the duo looked as small as ladybugs. For the first time she fully grasped the height she'd managed to climb and the true peril of this summit.

Diana stood and, glancing around, took in her surroundings. Flowers bloomed at her feet. She was in a small clearing surrounded by a thicket of woods. To her left, fifty yards away, she saw the pathway that led from the second plane up to the third. It was heavily guarded. Seven villagers paced the entrance, shovels and metal pitchforks gleaming in their hands. Straight across from Diana was a low stone fence that lined the edge of the forest, separating the woods from the town square. A fire crackled in a large stone pit in the center of town—she could make out the outlines of homes and shops around it. Diana shivered. The demon was likely nearby, lying in wait.

Diana scanned the trees closest to the cliff edge for vines. At last she found two, attached to a gnarly tree with low-hanging branches. She unwound the vines until she'd gathered enough length from each to reach the ground below. Then she hurriedly lowered both over the side, giving more slack until she felt a tug from each—Sakina and Augustus had grabbed hold. Digging her heels into the earth, Diana grasped one vine in each hand and pulled. Her arms strained. Her wrists ached. Looking over the edge, she saw Augustus and Sakina pulling themselves up. Sakina's face strained with the effort. Diana's own arms felt like they were being stretched to their very limits. But she thought of her mother, the enchanted women, and the demon and his cackling laughter. Diana pulled at the vines with everything she had, taking one backward step after another, until at last both Sakina and Augustus tumbled onto the grass.

Sakina's hair had come undone from her braid, falling messily around her shoulders. Augustus gulped in air and wiped his brow. They looked at her with wide eyes.

"Are you all right?" Diana asked softly. "Don't talk too loudly. We're pretty close to the town center."

"I'm okay. But you were amazing," Sakina said in a low voice. "You scampered up the cliff like it really was an olive tree on Themyscira."

"No one has ever done that before. Not *ever,*" said Augustus.

Diana glanced back at the cliff. It *was* a long way up, and it was dangerous. If she hadn't regained her footing after her one slip, she'd have been done for.

But she had found her toehold. She'd scaled the impossible.

"Well, the good news is that we're in the forest that houses the icta seed." Augustus looked at the firelit area in the distance and paused as he studied the men guarding the pathway to their left. "But the bad news is that the demon's likely on the other side of that clearing. Are the petals still in your ears?"

Diana grazed her ears with her fingers to check and nodded.

"Well, there's no time like the present to find the icta seed," Sakina said.

"Hold my water container?" Augustus turned to Sakina and handed it to her. "I can kneel better without it digging into my waist."

He dropped to his knees and began combing through the ivy coating the ground.

"What does its flower look like?" Sakina asked, kneeling next to him.

"It's purple and yellow," he told her. "Hard to make out in the dark, but there's definitely some around here."

"I'm going to approach the edge of town," Diana said. "See if I can locate where exactly this demon is lurking."

Mira swooped down and sat on Sakina's shoulder.

"Stay low," Sakina whispered to the bird. "When we need you, we'll call you. I don't want to risk your safety, understood?"

Mira chirped softly in response.

Diana tiptoed to the edge of the woods, which was lined with small, smooth gray boulders that formed a low decorative wall, stopping just at her knee. Taking care to stay hidden behind a tree, she took in the landscape. Augustus was right—the gods *had* paved the top plane completely flat. From this vantage point she could clearly see the town square, which was framed by a cobblestone street and quaint shops. There was a veterinary clinic. A tailoring shop. A bakery with a hanging wooden sign carved in the shape of a loaf of bread.

A bonfire crackled in the center of the square, and just then, something suddenly floated from behind a building and over to the flames.

Diana's stomach dropped.

She took a step backward.

Because there *he* was.

His back was toward her. The robe he wore hung loose and long. A sharp, jagged line of orange trailed from his head down the back of his robe. The skin on the back of his neck and his hands was translucent and pale. His body levitated inches above the ground. A vapor rose from his skin.

She held her breath. He was close, no more than five yards away. So close that even the smallest of movements could alert him to her presence.

Three brawny men carrying large, rusted pitchforks circled him slowly, their eyes blank. The rest of the villagers—some children as young as toddlers—stood motionless along the perimeter of the bonfire, waiting.

Diana glanced back at Sakina and Augustus. They waded through the ivy, frantically searching. Now that she knew where the demon was, she needed to join them and help find the final ingredient as quickly as possible. But before she could move a muscle, the demon swiveled toward her.

His eyes met Diana's.

His face broke into a wide, red smile.

"Why, hello there," he said. His voice was deep and gravelly. "I was wondering when you would arrive."

Chapter Twelve

Diana grew still. She stared at the hundreds of people who awaited his command, standing in even rows stretching four columns deep beneath the night sky. Save for the sound of flames flickering in the bonfire, silence filled the air.

"*Tsk, tsk.* Not very polite, are we?" The demon tilted his head. "When someone says hello, I do believe the correct protocol is to respond with a greeting in kind."

Diana's mouth felt as dry as sand. His words were muted because of the petals stuffing her ears; nevertheless, they chilled her to her core. The demon's eyes were gray and swirled like two dust storms in his pale, translucent face. Though he was a good five yards away, he seemed to tower over her. His lips were spread wider now. The hair on the back of her neck stood up. It was one thing to plan on defeating a demon to save Augustus's people and her own, but it was another thing entirely to look evil in the eye. What exactly were they up against?

"I must tell you," the demon continued, "you have managed to keep matters interesting for me. A remarkable endeavor, as I have seen a feat or two over my two centuries of living. But I confess that you will be my favorite capture thus far."

"Apparently I've kept matters so interesting that you actually *haven't* bothered to capture me yet," Diana responded coolly. She tried her best to keep her fear from showing, but his words shook her. *Two centuries of living?* Did she honestly believe that she, Augustus, and Sakina could truly destroy a creature that had managed to terrorize humans for that long?

"Not yet. You are a clever one, I shall grant you that much." The demon chuckled. "Perhaps it is why the reward for your capture was the highest he has ever offered."

"Reward?" Diana repeated slowly.

"Oh yes, a splendid one." The demon nodded. "Once I take you to him, he will be quite pleased, and you, my dear, will make me richer than I could have ever imagined."

"I'm not going anywhere with you."

"Oh, you most certainly will." His lips twisted into an ugly smile. "There are few things I am more certain of than this. And my townspeople here will be thrilled to ensure your compliance."

"They're not your townspeople! You're forcing them to do your work!" Sakina shouted from behind Diana. She rushed to Diana's side and put her arm tightly around her friend's shoulders. Her eyes blazed with anger.

"I would be careful how you speak to me if I were you." The demon's eyes narrowed. "And I must say, as pleased as I am that the boy delivered Diana like he promised, I could have done without the extra baggage. No matter. You can be taken care of easily enough."

Augustus. Diana turned her head slightly to check on him. The trees obscured him from the demon's view. Furiously, he ripped through the ivy, searching for the flower. Her heart raced. Clearly, he hadn't found it yet. And without its seed, they had no hope of destroying the demon.

"Thea." The demon snapped his fingers. "Over here."

A ginger-haired woman in a cotton dress stepped out of the line. She hurried over to him.

"How may I help you?" she asked in a wooden voice.

"It appears my work here is done. Be a dear and get my belongings. Package them properly, will you? I will be heading out shortly, with my bounty in tow."

The woman nodded, curtseyed, and hurried off.

"You both." He pointed to two motionless people standing in the crowd and snapped his fingers again. "Over here."

They stepped out of line and walked toward him, their eyes blank.

"After admiring your lovely chariots, I have

decided I would like one as well. The best you have. Preferably one encased in gold—the more luxurious, the better."

"We have only one in gold, sir," one of the men said flatly. "It belongs to the god of us all: Zeus."

"Ooh." The demon clasped his hands together. "Fit for *Zeus*? Even more thrilling. Yes, it will do nicely. Please prepare it for my departure, on the dock."

Diana stared at the demon, horrified. Most people trembled at the thought of facing Zeus for any wrongdoing. This demon was not just flagrantly disrespecting a city protected by the gods; he was now *stealing* from the gods. Zeus would not easily forgive this slight. Taking down the demon grew more and more urgent with each passing second. If he was bold enough to insult Zeus, what else was he capable of?

"Thank you for your help. You all are such an amiable lot." He smiled as the two men obediently trotted away for their mission.

"They're only listening to you because you've hypnotized them," Diana said.

"They may be hypnotized, you are correct. But you cannot deny they are content in obeying my orders."

He turned to the townsfolk and spoke again. "People of Sáz, your allegiance does not go unnoticed. You will certainly be rewarded for your assistance."

The townspeople mumbled their gratitude, their eyes fixed on empty space.

"You aren't going to win," Diana said. "This plan, whatever it is, will not work."

"But it already has." He laughed. "You are here, are you not?"

Diana clenched her fists. She hated how smug the demon looked.

"What do you want with me? Where do you want to take me?"

"You shall find out soon enough. Now, ah, let us proceed." He snapped his fingers a third time. "Follow along. Our chariot awaits."

"I'm not going anywhere with you," Diana responded. She planted her feet on the ground and crossed her arms.

"Perhaps I did not make myself clear." The demon cleared his throat. "Diana, the time has come for us to depart. Do follow me at once."

Diana watched him coolly. She felt grateful to Sakina for knowing exactly how to outsmart the demon's tactics and to Augustus for finding them petals to protect their hearing.

The demon frowned. And then he shrugged.

"Very well, then," he said. "If my words don't work on you—it happens at times—then never fear. I will simply capture you the old-fashioned way."

He moved toward her. The closer he floated, the more anger coursed through Diana's body. He was so arrogant and entitled, so certain he'd already triumphed. And the way he spoke about taking her with him, as though everyone were an object he could obtain or discard or use to his own advantage.

No. Diana clenched her jaw. He could not swoop in and claim her as a prize.

"You'll have to catch me first," she shouted. She glanced about for something—anything—to throw at him and noticed a boulder, loosened from the fence. Gripping it, she heaved it up and hurled it at the demon. The rock flew through the air, whizzing toward him—and passed straight through the demon's torso and out the other side, landing with a sharp crack on the street beyond the bonfire. The demon glanced down at his midsection and then up at her. His face broke into a grin—and then he roared with laughter.

"Impressive toss. From where I stand, the boulder looked quite heavy. Though I suppose looks can be deceiving if a girl as little as you could lift it so handily."

Diana glared at him. She was still afraid of him and all that he could do, but she longed desperately to wipe the smug expression off his face.

She glanced into the woods. Augustus no longer sifted through the grassy floor. Instead, he stood straight as the trees. Their eyes met. Imperceptibly, he nodded.

He had found the seed!

Diana fidgeted. It was one thing to have all the ingredients, but that meant nothing if they weren't combined at the exact right time. But how were they going to complete the potion under the demon's watchful eye? She could grab the canteen from Sakina and run to Augustus. She'd be there in a matter of seconds, but the mushroom wasn't something they could simply grab and toss into the canteen. It required care and caution. Even one small mistake could ruin their plan completely.

"Now, as for you," the demon hissed, his gaze turning to Sakina. "Listen to me, girl." The amusement in his voice was gone. He snapped his fingers once more. "There is a jagged cliff beyond the tree line. Take a leap off it."

"I'm not doing anything you tell me to do." Sakina glowered at him.

"Hmm. Dance," he ordered, snapping his fingers again. "Turn in a circle four times."

Augustus gingerly moved through the woods toward them, but he was still far. Too far. Diana tried to keep her eyes trained on the demon so he wouldn't notice Augustus inching closer.

"Stuffed your ears, eh?" the demon said, recognition flickering in his face as he studied both girls. "Common trick. No matter, though. There are other means. Brutus—come here. Get rid of that girl over there, would you?"

Sakina's eyes widened. Before she could say anything, another voice cried out.

"No!" Augustus gasped. The man approaching them was thin, his shoulders rounded. Blond hair swept his forehead.

Diana winced. Augustus was meant to stay hidden. How else would they stealthily mix the ingredients? But it was too late. The demon's eyes were fixed on Augustus now.

"Well, well, well, if it isn't the man of the hour." The demon stared at Augustus and grinned. "I must admit, I was of two minds about whether you were up to the task. You performed remarkably."

"You gave me no choice," Augustus shouted.

"Choice!" The demon threw his head back and scoffed. "Completely overrated. Now, Brutus." He snapped his fingers. "The girl. Get on with it. Toss her over the cliff. I think that's the simplest solution."

Sakina trembled like a leaf in a storm. Diana

jumped in front of her. No one was laying a hand on her best friend.

"Father," Augustus cried out. "Don't do this!"

His father?

Augustus rushed toward the man, passing Diana and Sakina.

"It's me." Augustus tugged on his father's arm, though Brutus continued stalking toward Diana and Sakina. "It's Auggie. Please don't listen to this demon! He's evil!"

"Evil?" The demon's eyes glinted. "Now that hurts my feelings. Truly. I am here to help your village, to give you order and purpose. How is this evil?"

"It's not true, Father! You can't trust anything he says!" Augustus shoved at his father, pushing him, trying to get him to stop his relentless walk toward Sakina. "You're better than this, Father. You're strong! You can ignore him. Please, try!"

The demon glared at Augustus. "On second thought, Brutus, why don't you go ahead and get the boy first. After some consideration, I've decided to take him with me and keep him for myself," the demon continued. "His potion making and chariot construction skills will be useful to me."

"Yes, sir," the man said blankly.

"Father." Augustus's lower lip quivered. He backed away. "I'm your son. Your only child. Don't you see me?"

"He sees only the being he serves," the demon responded. "And for that he shall be richly rewarded."

But there were no rewards. Brutus was ready to send his own son off with the demon, to give him away as a slave. How did all these people believe the demon's lies, ignoring what they were witnessing with their own eyes?

Diana straightened suddenly. *That's it!* She had to help the townspeople see *exactly* who they were dealing with. They needed to hear the truth from the demon himself. Then maybe the truth would set them free. She glanced at the lasso tied to her belt. Augustus's hesitation might be right—the lasso might not work on someone made of vapor—but their options were running out. If she could get it around the demon and make him confess that he'd hypnotized the people of Sáz, the spell could be undone entirely, setting the entire island free. A boulder didn't do anything, but perhaps the lasso could!

She yanked the lasso from her belt, but before she could make a move, a rustling noise sounded behind her.

Augustus's eyes widened and he screamed, "Watch out!"

Chapter Thirteen

Quickly, Diana turned toward the sound. Men—the same ones who'd been patrolling the second plane—were appearing from the pathway on their left, walking past the motionless guards and marching in lockstep toward the girls. Their bodies moved stiffly but purposefully, blocking any path of escape in that direction.

"We have to fight them!" Augustus clenched his palms into fists. Before he could do anything, his father snatched him from the ground by the scruff of his collar, locking him in a choke hold.

"Father—please!" Augustus spluttered. He coughed and kicked his feet furiously. His face grew pink and flustered. But Brutus seemed more like a stone wall than a person—he didn't react to his son's cries, and his arms stayed firmly wrapped around Augustus's body.

Until tonight Diana had never realized how terrifying a blank expression could be. These people followed orders without any thought or reaction to what was being demanded of them. They had no emotions. They could kill her or Sakina, or even Augustus, without blinking. In their hypnotized state, there was nothing the townsfolk wouldn't do for the demon. It was chilling to be surrounded by people who no longer had a concept of what was right and what was wrong—people whose humanity had been simply erased.

"Let's head to the left!" Diana said, scanning their surroundings in the darkness. They hadn't mixed the potion yet. Sakina had the canteen, but Augustus had two critical ingredients with him, and there was no way they'd get them now, with him trapped so firmly in his father's grip. They had to run, to hide until they could figure out what to do next.

But before she could move, villagers began stepping out of the silent rows lining the town square.

They marched forward, more and more of them, until they formed a wall between the girls, the village, and the forest on either side. They all held an assortment of knives: jagged butcher blades, carving knives, and metal saws. Some clutched swords with steel edges, long and pointed. Others clutched metal rods or pitchforks.

"We're . . . we're surrounded," Sakina whispered.

Fear pounded through Diana's veins. Sakina was right. The towering cliff they'd climbed was at their backs. There was nowhere to escape. The villagers would bear down upon them until they were captured.

"Why aren't they moving? They're just staring at us," Sakina said slowly. She gestured to the motionless people.

"They're waiting for the demon," Diana said. "They need him to give the order."

"And then?" Sakina's voice trembled. "What do we do?"

Beads of sweat trailed down Diana's forehead. She didn't want to do this. But the truth was unavoidable. There was only one thing they *could* do. She pulled out her sword and tightly gripped its hilt.

"You presume to think you can fight your way out?" The demon chuckled. He watched them from beside the glowing bonfire at the town's center. The corners of his lips curled into a sinister smile. "I must confess: I am not typically a fan of theatrics, but this is quite entertaining. A pity all good things must eventually come to an end."

With one hand, he snapped his fingers.

"Get them," he growled.

The crowd of people surrounding the girls straightened. Their jaws tensed. And then, slowly, they began approaching, the circle of people shrinking inward toward Diana and Sakina with each step until they stood only a few feet away. Their weapons were held aloft, angled to point to the ground or sticking straight up in the air. Their grips were clumsy, hesitant.

Diana smiled a little. Finally, a glimmer of hope! The demon could hypnotize the villagers to obey him, but he couldn't teach them how to fight. They had no idea how to even hold their weapons. Diana and Sakina had a chance!

Diana turned her head and whispered to Sakina, "These people are *not* fighters, remember?"

"Maybe. But a weapon is still a weapon," Sakina responded shakily. "And we're outnumbered."

"It's not all about numbers. We're not defenseless. Keep your weapon drawn and ready. When I say the word, we strike."

"Strike? I just got this sword a week before our trip! I'm not even sure if I know how to chop an apple with it!" Sakina whisper-shouted frantically.

"There's a first time for everything. We can do this," Diana assured her. "We're going to defend ourselves, but we're going to take care not to kill anyone. Draw your weapon. Stay close. Press your back to mine. We can't get separated, not for a second."

Diana tried her best to mask her own fears. Though she'd practiced in secret from time to time and had watched the Amazon warriors sparring and fighting since she was little, this was her first time actually defending herself with a weapon. And this situation was trickier than most: Though the people who lumbered toward them meant her and Sakina harm, their minds had been hijacked by the demon. They couldn't control their actions. Not only did Diana need to defend herself, but she also needed to make sure she didn't hurt anyone too seriously. These were innocent people—none of them deserved to die, even if they came hard at Diana and Sakina.

The townsfolk inched closer. Their black-laced boots rose and fell steadily in unison until they formed a tight circle around the girls. One man stepped forward. He had a straw hat and skinny arms and carried a sword with a gleaming blade. The weapon trembled in his grasp. Diana had no doubt that she could fight him off, but making sure she didn't gravely injure him in the process would be a challenge. Approaching her, the man reached out a hand to grab her arm.

It's time.

Channeling her Amazon warrior roots, Diana gripped her weapon tightly, locked her knees, and swung her sword against his. The blades clanked violently against each other, the noise a shock in the still night. The man spun from the impact. His sword fell to the ground.

For a moment, no one moved. Then the villagers' heads swiveled in unison toward the fallen man.

"Get them!" shouted the demon. "Now. Do not stop until they are disbanded and captured."

More townsfolk jumped from the circle and approached the girls from either side. Many of them were taller than the previous man, and every one had arms bulging with muscles.

"Jump and kick!" Diana shouted to Sakina. "Aim with the strongest parts of your body against their weakest!"

Diana planted her feet on the dirt beneath her and then, with a grunt, she propelled herself off the ground and spun. She attacked the man in front of her with a roundhouse kick to his upper chest. He tumbled backward. Another man ran toward her—Diana deployed the same move, knocking him down with one kick.

"Just follow my lead until they're all down!" Diana yelled at Sakina.

"Okay," said Sakina breathlessly. "I will. . . . NO!"

A man with a thick mustache ran full speed toward Sakina. Before she could jump out of the way, he swiped a leg at her brown leather boots, catching her behind the knees. Sakina tripped and fell, slamming to the ground. The man grabbed both of her feet and began dragging her away. Sakina's body bumped and thudded against tree roots and across overgrown vines. She tried twisting her body to strike behind her but lashed her sword at him in vain.

Diana hurried after her friend but was stopped when strong arms sprang around her from behind. One arm clamped around Diana's neck and she was lifted into the air by her throat. Diana coughed and wheezed, her breathing growing strained. The hold pressed tighter against her windpipe. Stars began to dance in and out of Diana's vision. She scrambled against the grip, her nails scratching into flesh. *I'm going to pass out,* she thought frantically.

Diana thought of Antiope and the lessons she'd learned. She closed her eyes and strained against the arm. She needed to dig deeper within herself than she ever had before. She couldn't lose hope. A burst of dizziness made the world spin, and darkness entered her vision. With all her might, Diana slammed her legs backward with full force against the townsperson's shins.

Their hands sprang away as the person fell backward, landing with a thud on the ground.

Diana's eyes watered from the tight hold and her neck throbbed with pain, but there was no time to waste—Sakina was ten feet away and growing farther still as the man dragged her past the other townsfolk and into the forest. Diana realized with a start that they were almost at the edge of the cliff—and that he was going to *throw her off it.*

Pumping her fists, Diana raced between the trees, deftly dodging other townspeople as she ran. The man's body was hunched over as he dragged Sakina. Once Diana was close enough, she reared her leg as far back as she could and then flung her foot up hard, like a whip, kicking his shoulder. The man staggered. One hand flew to the shoulder where she'd struck him, but the other remained firm around Sakina's ankle.

"My turn!" Sakina shouted. She flipped onto her back and flicked her sword up. Swinging with all her strength, her face contorted, she sliced at the man's hand and arm until he yelped and released his grip on her leg.

Sakina sprang up and hurried to Diana. They rushed away from the looming cliff. Clutching his wrist, the man broke into a run, following them. Diana turned and pulled out her lasso. She snapped it, and the rope smacked the man in the head. He staggered and fell to the ground.

"There's a gap!" Diana pointed to an unguarded opening to their left. "Are you okay to run?"

"Yes! Let's do it!" Sakina said.

Picking up their pace, they hurried through the trees. At last they spotted a dirt path trailing through ancient trees, leading out of the woods. Diana and Sakina followed the path, but as they approached, the leaves began to rustle. Two men swung down from branches, aiming at Diana and Sakina. The girls ducked and dodged, missing the blows by a few inches.

More people lay in wait, hidden among the

moonlit foliage and in the trees lining the path. Leather-booted feet dangled from the branches where townsfolk sat among the tree branches.

A woman leapt down from a flowering evergreen to Diana's left. She huffed and ran full speed at the girls, as though planning to mow them over with her body. Diana crouched, and once the woman was close enough, Diana raised her leg and kicked her in the shoulder. The woman's head slammed against a tree, she fell, and then she grew still. Diana flinched, hoping the woman would be okay.

"They won't stop." Sakina choked back tears, her eyes frantically scanning the horizon. "They keep coming. It's never going to end, is it?"

Diana glanced at the town square in the distance behind them. Rows of people stretched out far beyond the girl's line of sight. Their frames formed long shadows from the bonfire crackling nearby. Six more men hurried out of the rows as Diana watched. They wore peasant shirts and dirty linen pants.

"We need to outrun them and regroup to plan the next strategy," Diana said. "It's our only—"

She stopped with a start and bit her lip. The

demon appeared to be two steps ahead of them. A group of villagers approached the path from ahead, blocking it. Pitchforks burned in their hands. The other group of six men grew closer and closer to the girls.

"They're everywhere. And we can't take on multiple people with weapons all at once, Diana." Sakina shook her head. "It's impossible."

Diana had seen the women back home practice scenarios like this—surrounded by even more enemies than this and winning nonetheless—countless times. But it was one thing to watch others do something and another to do it herself, especially during a matter of life and death. Diana took a deep breath and steeled her resolve. She had no idea if she could do it. But she knew they had to try.

Gripping her sword, she tensed as the men grew closer. Sakina stood so closely next to her that their shoulders brushed. Fallen twigs snapped beneath the villagers' feet. They were in striking range now. Diana clenched her jaw and raised her sword in the air. And then she spun. With the speed of a fluttering hummingbird, Diana twirled and sliced her sword hard against the men's weapons. More and more approached. Diana didn't stop. She struck with her elbow against their heads. She kicked them in the shins.

At last their weapons fell to the ground. The men, now unarmed, wheezed and panted, bending at the waist, gulping for air. But then they straightened again. Bruises lined their bodies. Their shirts were ripped, their pants torn. Nevertheless, they formed clumsy fists with their hands and ambled toward the girls.

"How can they keep going?" Sakina said. "Their bodies can't possibly take any more."

"The demon told them not to stop until they got us," Diana replied. "They'll keep going until they physically can't."

Even now, as they prepared to attack the girls yet again, Diana couldn't help but feel sorry for them. They weren't acting of their own free will. They were just the demon's tools.

Diana tucked her sword back in her belt. She was

not about to attack unarmed people with a sword, even if they were trying to capture her. She clenched her fists. And then as the villagers neared, Diana leapt in the air and swiveled her arm. She struck the edge of her elbow against the first man's head. He crumpled to the ground.

"Sakina!" Diana shouted as another person rushed toward her friend. "Give them a power-angle kick! Crack your leg like a whip against their body—aim for their shins!"

"You got it!" Sakina grunted. She leapt and kicked against their legs with her boots. The person stumbled backward, their hands releasing from Diana.

"That—was—awesome," Diana breathed out. She leapt and pushed another person in the chest, sending them tumbling to the ground.

"Learning from the best," Sakina replied.

They ducked and kicked and fought.

Diana bent her knee for a front leg kick, and toppled another man coming at her. He flew back, thudding against a tree before falling unconscious.

Somewhere in the distant depths of Diana's mind, she knew this was an impossible feat—fighting off dozens of armed men nearly twice her size—and yet here she was. And though her heart raced, her mind felt clear and sure. She was fighting like the warrior she had always believed she was meant to be.

"To your left!" Sakina shouted.

The last of the villagers approached Diana. Twisting her body to gain speed, Diana spun into the air and kicked out her foot, landing it against the man's torso with such force that he fell to the ground, knocked out.

And then it was over.

"You did it." Sakina gasped for air. "You really did it."

"*We* did it." Diana winced at the fresh new bruise on Sakina's cheek. Her leggings had torn at the knees. "You okay?"

"Better than they are," Sakina replied.

The villagers lay curled on the ground. Some were still passed out; others moaned, their eyes shut, cradling their legs or arms.

The demon floated toward them in the woods. He crossed his arms. The smug expression on his face from earlier was replaced with one of profound irritation. Brutus walked beside the demon, Augustus still firmly in his clutches.

"Your skills are impressive. However, you fail to grasp a fundamental point," the demon said. "There are only two of you. And hundreds of people are on my side. Sooner or later, I will win."

"Try harder, then," Diana said through gritted teeth. His arrogance made her blood boil.

"Very well," the demon said. His lips pressed into a thin straight line. He turned toward the remaining crowd of stock-still people waiting in a motionless line, visible through the tree line. He snapped his fingers. "Marco, finish this once and for all."

"No," whimpered Augustus. He strained against his father's grip.

Diana drew a sharp intake of breath as Marco emerged from the crowd and walked toward them. Marco was tall, practically the same height as the demon himself, broad-shouldered, and lean. He held no weapons. He didn't need them; his body *was* the weapon.

"I don't even know how to get around him,"

Sakina whispered. "There *are* two of us, but . . ." Her voice trailed off.

Sakina was right. This man was too big to swing a sword at and hope to win.

"We could try to run?" Sakina whispered. "He is stronger, but we might be faster."

Diana swallowed. They could run. But for how long? There were hundreds of townsfolk. The demon wouldn't stop. He'd never give up. She stepped back as the man lumbered closer. She'd taken out a lot of people tonight, but this man was different. He looked as strong as an ox. He might not know how to fight, but he wouldn't need to—he had pure brute strength on his side.

Diana glanced at her belt. The lasso.

This was it!

Perhaps the demon was too far away to corral with the Lasso of Truth, but in a few more paces, Marco would be right in the line of capture. She could lasso him in, and maybe it would break his spell. She could force him to speak the truth of what was happening—the lasso could help him see.

"Stand down," Diana told Sakina. "Lower your weapon. Let him come to us."

The man continued toward them with expressionless eyes. His jaw was slack, but his fists were clenched. Diana shivered. Once he was arm's length away, she pulled out the Lasso of Truth and swung it toward him. It landed in a perfect arc around his middle.

Marco frowned at the rope settling around his torso. He jerked to tear it off. But then the lasso glimmered and glowed. He blinked, and his hands fell to his side.

"What . . . what is happening?" he asked, glancing around in astonishment. "Why am I out here at this time of night?" Looking at Diana and then at Sakina, he blinked in confusion. "Who are you?"

"Marco!" Augustus cried out. "You have to help us. Please!"

The man started at the sight of Augustus, who was clamped tightly around the waist by his father.

"Brutus," Marco croaked. "What are you doing to your little boy? What is going on?"

"Enough questions!" the demon shouted. "End it! Get the girl."

"This demon is controlling our entire town," Augustus said. His eyes filled with tears. "He's been terrorizing us since yesterday." He gestured to Diana. "He sent me on a mission to kidnap her. This thing is evil. We have to destroy him."

"The boy lies," the demon said coolly. "I am here to help. To give you more than you can imagine. The girl fetches a large price. And for your help, I will repay you all handsomely and you will share in my wealth. You will never want for anything again."

"We don't need anything from *you,*" Augustus shouted.

Marco stared at the boy and then at Diana. And then he turned to the demon.

"This girl is a child. What on earth do you want with her?"

"That is my business. Yours is to do as you're told."

"I don't take orders from anyone." Marco shot the demon an angry look. "What makes you think you can come into our town and tell us what to do?"

"I would be careful speaking to me in this way. *Someone* will get these girls," the demon said, "and for them there will be a most wonderful reward."

Marco studied the demon. And then his eyes narrowed.

"If you think you can barge into our town and tell us what's what, you've got another thing coming."

The demon glared at Marco. And then he lifted a hand above his head. He snapped his fingers once more. With a deep growl, he bellowed:

"Now!"

Augustus's eyes widened—but before he could speak, Brutus clamped a hand over his son's mouth.

The next thing Diana heard was movement, rustling through trees behind them. And then a gang of people rushing toward her, Sakina, and Marco. Each of them held thick clubs. Before she could jump out of the way, the biggest of them was upon her. A giant club swung toward her head.

Pain seared through Diana's skull. In one quick, horrifying moment, everything faded to black.

Chapter Fourteen

The first sensations Diana felt when she came to were the dirt beneath her face and then a deep, dull throbbing at the base of her neck. She moved to touch this sore spot, but her hand caught against something. Glancing down, she gasped. Her wrists were clamped together with cold metal cuffs and firmly chained to an iron stake in the ground. They'd captured her.

They'd gotten Sakina, too. She lay steps away from Diana, chained to another stake. She had a fresh new bruise on her face and a welt across her forehead. Her mouth was parted, her eyes closed. Was she passed out, or was she . . . ? Diana's eyes welled with tears. She couldn't finish the thought.

Sakina *had* to be okay. Straining against the chains, Diana tried inching closer to her friend, but the thick steel refused to give.

Tears trailed down Augustus's cheeks. His father still grasped him firmly. Marco stood next to the demon. A red gash slashed across his arm and his chin. Gone was his wide-eyed bewilderment; his eyes were blank. The enchantment was once again rooted in his mind. Three villagers stood a few steps from the bonfire, closer to where Diana lay, their eyes fixed on her. Diana recognized that she was in the town square.

"Up from your little nap?" the demon asked Diana. She couldn't tell how long she'd been passed out, but it was still dark. The demon floated toward her until he hovered mere inches away. Steam and heat emanated from his body. A glimmer of something in his hand caught her eye. Diana felt the color leave her face.

It was the Lasso of Truth.

He followed her gaze. "This is quite the nifty little device. I have heard legends of it but never knew it was genuine until tonight. It is not much use to me—twisting the truth is far more useful than drawing it out—but I am certain it will fetch a good sum in the marketplace."

"Let. Me. Go." Diana gritted her teeth and pulled at the chains.

He watched her strain against her binding. "I admire your spirit," he said. "But I must tell you, there is the quality of not going down without a fight, and then there is the other bit about knowing when to quit."

"This isn't over."

"You are keeping it interesting, I will grant you that much. My trickiest catch so far, and considering how long I have been in the business, this is saying something. And at least now I can say I earned my bounty in full." The demon glanced at Augustus and grinned. "And I get an errand boy all my own to build and make potions for me. It is what you might call a win-win-win."

"I will never work for you," Augustus spat. His face was pinched and angry. "Never."

"Once we pluck out whatever is clogging up your ears, you most certainly will." He nodded to Brutus.

"Go on, then. Pull it out. What exactly do you have stuffed in there? I must say I have seen the most amusing items over the years."

Brutus held the struggling boy and yanked the petals from Augustus's ears. They fluttered to the ground.

"I will never listen to you!" Augustus shouted. "Never!"

"Flower petals? Well, this is a first." The demon chuckled. "Your creativity will certainly prove useful. And now that we have dispensed with the dramatics, let us get on with the hypnotism, shall we?" The demon approached Augustus. "I am here to help you and your people. You are very grateful I have arrived, I see."

The boy stood tense and then his jaw slackened. The furrow in his brow smoothed.

"Very grateful," Augustus said stoically.

"Augustus, no!" Diana cried out. But it was too late. Faster than she could imagine, the demon had taken control of him.

"I am most pleased that you will accompany me to my land. You will help me with potions and serve as my own personal chariot maker. And I am certain your carpentry skills will be useful to me in other ways as well. Doesn't that sound fun?"

"Fun," the boy repeated. His shoulders drooped.

Diana's heart twisted. Augustus still stood before her, but in the real sense he was gone.

"Now I suppose I *could* remove your petals, too," the demon mused, studying Diana. "Though I think—"

A silver flash streaked suddenly through the air. *Mira!* She flew through the darkness and dove at the demon. The demon slashed his hands in front of him, the gray in his eyes darkening. Mira furiously pecked at him with her beak but ended up flying through him instead. She circled overhead and let out a great screech. With the moonlight shining down, Diana could see why she'd screamed: the bird had been singed along her tail and wings due to her act of heroism.

"Do my eyes deceive me, or was that truly a gamma gazelle?" the demon mused as he peered into the darkness. "What a marvel of fortune this day is turning out to be. I must have it. A rare demon ought to have a rare bird." He turned to a teenage boy standing by the fire pit. "You have only one task: get the bird and bring it to me. Failure is not an option."

"Yes, sir," he mumbled. He hurried into the night.

"You can't enchant a bird," Diana said. "She'll never belong to you."

"In a cage she does not get much of a say, now does she? And if she proves herself to be inconvenient company, I can always sell her for a fair price." The demon shrugged. "Either way, I win."

The demon swirled closer to Diana.

"I'd think twice before you lay a hand on me," Diana warned as he neared.

"Worry not," the demon smirked. "No harm shall come to you. You are wanted as unscathed as possible in order for me to collect your full price."

Diana shivered; the glowering demon was an evil-enough entity, but a danger far more mysterious lurked somewhere—a being who had gone to untold lengths in order to have her captured alive.

"What would you like me to do with this girl?"

Marco asked. He pointed to Sakina. She still lay unconscious.

"Pay her no mind. She can burn with the rest of the village. It is what you all want, is it not?" He glanced at the villagers. "Burning is a rebirth. I am sure you all will welcome it."

"What?" Diana's mouth went dry. "You swore you wouldn't. You promised you'd leave them alone if they did what you said! You said you'd reward them!"

"What can I say?" The demon shrugged. "Demons are not known for keeping their word. And me? I am a master of lies."

Diana scanned the crowd of people, hoping this piece of information would jar at least *someone's* attention. This demon was casually discussing killing them, burning their homes! But no one reacted. The hypnotism turned off any ability for them to think for themselves.

"The people here are chariot makers for the gods," Diana said. "Do you think the gods will look kindly upon someone who has destroyed the people they were entrusted to protect? Do you have any idea what they will do to you?"

"The gods," the demon snarled. His expression darkened. "They think they know everything. Everyone trembles, fearing they might grow angry. Not me. They may be powerful, but I? I am far more clever than they."

"They'll catch you. Sooner or later they will," Diana said, "and when they do, they'll make you pay for what you've done."

"The gods will never know what happened. We will not leave any evidence behind. He was clear on this point."

"Who is *he*?" Diana shouted. "Who is the being who wants to kidnap me? What will he do to me? I have a right to know!"

"It will all be attributed to a brush fire," the demon continued, ignoring Diana. "Or a lightning strike. Happens all the time. An unavoidable tragedy. But for the best, yes, Augustus and Brutus?"

"For the best," the man repeated.

"For the best." Augustus nodded placidly.

Diana swallowed and fought back tears. Seeing

Augustus succumb so completely was heartbreaking. He'd had so much fight in him before now. The demon was a *monster.*

"Take torches and light them in the bonfire," the demon instructed the people of the town. "Hold them at the ready, and wait for my signal. Once we lift off in the chariot, start torching from the center of town and work your way outward."

Diana watched the lines of motionless people mechanically retrieve torches and light them.

"As soon as I have the bird, we shall depart," the demon said. "In the meantime—you, boy," he hissed at Augustus. "Do you have a store of potions?"

"Yes," said Augustus in a stilted voice. "Thousands."

"Thousands, you say?" the demon asked. "Surely I have no use for all of them, but take me to where you keep them. I will determine which ones suit my needs best; no sense in letting perfectly good potions go to waste. And you three"—he pointed to the three guards watching Diana and Sakina—"keep an eye on the villagers lighting the torches. When I give the word, pull the stake out and carry

Diana down to the runway. But keep her chained until I say so. She is a slippery one.

"And now I must bid you adieu, Diana." The demon shot her a wicked smile. "But fear not—our parting shall not be for long. We will meet again very soon."

And with that, the demon slipped away, Augustus by his side. She watched as the demon's figure grew more and more distant down the cobblestone road until they turned a corner and were gone. She looked at her guards—their backs were turned to her, their eyes trained on where the demon had disappeared from sight.

Diana glared at the empty space where he had stood. The demon was preparing to leave. He planned to hand her over to a mysterious figure who was willing to destroy hundreds of lives just to possess her.

He had won.

No.

Diana clenched her jaw. She strained against the chains binding her.

He was not going to kidnap her.

He would not steal Mira.

He was not going to kill Sakina.

Or enslave Augustus.

And he was certainly *not* going to destroy this village and all who were within it.

Diana pulled at her handcuffs with everything she had. She strained against the metal. Her face flushed like a fever as she ground her teeth together. She struggled against the cuffs until her wrists turned bright red. The steel dug into her hands and pain pulsed through her body, but Diana didn't stop. And then—

Diana blinked. The world began spinning. It was as though time was both hurtling forward at hyperspeed and slowing down all in the same breath.

Bearing down, Diana twisted against the metal with all her might. The pain had vanished.

And then—a crack.

The metal cuffs split in half. Diana looked down at her hands.

She was *free.*

Chapter Fifteen

Breathlessly, Diana scrambled to her friend's side. She pinched her fingers against the metal of Sakina's handcuffs and, with all her strength, yanked. The cuffs fell apart like glass bangles.

"Please be alive. Please be alive," Diana murmured like a prayer under her breath. She placed a finger on her friend's neck and felt weak with relief at the steady pulsing beat.

The guards stood by the bonfire, awaiting the next order. Their backs were to the girls. Twisting off the top of her water canteen, Diana gingerly poured some water into her palm and then splashed Sakina. It worked; Sakina's eyes sprang open. She sat up and flinched, gingerly touching the welt growing on her forehead.

"What happened?" Sakina croaked softly. "My head feels so heavy."

"We got knocked out," Diana whispered. She glanced at the guards, but they remained distracted. "They ambushed us. But you're okay."

"You broke me out of *handcuffs*?" Sakina stared at the broken metal bits on the ground. "They're made of metal."

"I don't know how it happened," Diana said. The reality of what she'd done settled in on her. It should have been impossible to break out of those cuffs. And yet—she'd done it.

"Where's Augustus?" Sakina asked. "Is he . . . ? Is he . . . ?"

"The demon has him," Diana said. She glanced furtively at the guards. "He's hypnotized."

"No." Sakina clasped her hands to her mouth.

"He took Augustus to gather potions at his workshop. Once the demon picks the ones he wants, we're going to the runway."

"But Augustus has the mushroom and the seed! I have the canteen, but we can't do anything to the demon without those two ingredients."

"Maybe we could get them from his pouch somehow."

"How? He's enchanted!"

"Still," Diana said, "there has to be a way. We can figure something out. Let's head to the runway and wait for them. At least then we'll be one step ahead."

There was a rustle in the trees and then Mira flew toward them. She swooped and settled on Sakina's shoulder.

"Oh, Mira." Sakina breathed a sigh of relief. But then she paused, taking in Mira's singed feathers. "What happened here?"

"She tried saving us," Diana told her. "She dove at the demon and got burned flying through him."

"Poor thing," Sakina said softly to Mira. "Thank you for trying."

Diana nodded to the bird. "She's the one buying us a little extra time. He wants to capture Mira and take her with him as a pet. I'm supposedly making him richer than he ever could have imagined, but that's still not enough. What does a demon even *want* with money?"

"No kidding," Sakina murmured. "His greed knows no bounds, does it?"

Diana sat up straighter. The demon *was* greedy. He wanted more and more. And right now he wanted Mira. Maybe that was the key! They could use his greed against him by distracting him with the newest thing he wanted: Mira.

"That's it!" she exclaimed.

"What is?" Sakina asked.

"His fixation!" She looked at the bird. "If Mira is up for another act of bravery, maybe we have a shot at destroying him."

"What did you have in mind?" Sakina asked.

"Mira can lure him. Distract him," Diana explained. "We'll hide in the woods while she flies to where he is—not close enough to get caught but close enough to keep his eyes off Augustus. While he's busy trying to trap Mira, one of us can reach Augustus and get the rest of the ingredients."

"Even if Mira *is* able to distract the demon," Sakina said slowly, "what if Augustus won't help us? If the demon tells him to hurt us, he will."

"I know. But we do know way more combat techniques than he does," Diana said. "If we absolutely need to, we could take him on."

"And the potion." Sakina bit her lip. "It'll work, won't it?"

"It has to," Diana said, grim.

She wished there was a less risky way, but this looked like the best chance they had.

"Do you think you can distract the demon?" Sakina asked Mira. "We'll need to make sure he moves far away from Augustus."

"I know this is a huge risk," Diana said. "I understand if she doesn't want to."

The bird swirled in the air.

"She's in," Sakina said.

Both girls rose from the ground. They took one step toward the forest. Just then the ground thudded beneath their feet. Diana looked up with a start.

"What was that?" Sakina said slowly.

Looking toward the bonfire, the girls saw the

townspeople—every last one, even the children—moving toward them. Some held burning torches. Others had clenched fists. Their faces were blank, their eyes unfocused. They took a step forward in unison. And then another. And then, like a wave, they charged toward Sakina and Diana.

Diana glanced at Sakina.

She shouted one word:

"Run!"

Chapter Sixteen

Run.

The three-letter word thumped through Diana's body like a heartbeat.

The girls raced down the path leading to the second plane of flowering meadows and the river of lava. The villagers stayed fast on their heels, and though the girls ran with all their might, the townspeople were catching up.

"They know—this place—better than us," Sakina panted. They hurried past the trees and through the wildflowers. "How do we—outrun—hundreds of—people?"

Diana whipped her head around, weighing the possibilities. They could hide in the hollowed-out tree or try to fight them one-on-one. But there were too many of them. She and Sakina couldn't take on everyone themselves.

"We may not be able to outrun them," Diana said, brightening, "but we *can* try to outmaneuver them. It's darker here because of all the trees, and they're moving awkwardly because of the hypnotism anyway, so it's possible they could lose their bearings. They could get caught in the traps!"

"And what about us?" Sakina asked. "They're not exactly simple traps—we may not be able to avoid them, either!"

"We have something they don't. We have Mira."

Mira sped toward them, flying low, her eyes shooting beams into the night. The girls followed her and ran. They hopped over metal jaws, ducked beneath leaves and branches that hid nets.

Sweat trickled down Diana's brow. Despite how quickly she and Sakina raced past the traps, the villagers weren't slowing their pace.

That is, they weren't slowed until the girls hopped over a hidden net. Diana heard the snapping sound of restraints uncoiling. A voice cried out, then grew muffled. Diana's body shuddered with relief and regret that a trap had finally been deployed against a villager, but she didn't slow her pace.

"Got ya!" a man grunted close behind them. He leapt over a ditch, pumping his arms at full speed, overtaking the girls.

"Jump!" Diana shouted to her friend. Both girls leapt over a metal jaw glinting through a pile of leaves. The man was not so lucky. His foot caught against the trap and the jaw clamped shut, its teeth sinking into his ankle. The man screamed and fell to the ground.

With each step the girls took, more and more cries filled the forest as people were caught in nets or tumbled into darkened pits.

After what felt like forever as they ran without pause, the sounds stopped. The ground was no longer vibrating with the sound of thundering footsteps. The girls slowed down, breathing hard. They turned back. No one followed them anymore.

"I think—they're—gone," Sakina said breathlessly. Mira fluttered and sat on her shoulder. "I think—they—"

Just then a scrawny teenager with gleaming blue eyes crept out from behind a tree and lunged at Sakina.

Sakina jumped back—but he wasn't after her. His gaze was solidly fixed on Mira; Diana recognized him as the boy specifically ordered to hunt the bird. The teen lashed his hands out, trying to grab Mira. The bird screeched, then flew above the tree line and out of sight.

The girls watched the teenager race after the bird, disappearing into the darkness.

"Don't worry," Diana said gently. "Only one of them can fly."

Sakina nodded slowly, but Diana saw the concern lining her face.

The girls headed toward the shore, where the runway and the dock lay parallel to one another. They stopped just at the tree line. Clouds brewed overhead—the rumblings of a storm echoed in the distance. The beach was a few dozen steps away, the dock and runway not far from where they stood. A brilliant golden chariot with silver engravings was perched on the runway to their left. It glittered silver beneath the moonlight shining directly overhead. Waves crashed restlessly against the beach and the boulders lining the shores. The demon and Augustus stood before the chariot on the runway.

"Very nice, Augustus," the demon's gravelly voice rasped. "The craftsmanship of your people is truly unrivaled."

Diana fidgeted and looked up through the trees. Where was Mira? They needed her here to distract the demon.

Sakina bit her lip.

"She'll be here soon," Diana whispered. "No one can catch Mira. I know it."

But minutes passed by. And then several more. Mira still did not appear.

"Do you think she got trapped?" Sakina whispered. "There's no other explanation. She'd be here if something hadn't happened." She shook her head. "I can't let her be trapped again. Not like last time. The merchant she belonged to before was evil . . . but this will be far worse."

Tears formed in Diana's eyes. She didn't want to believe it, but it was true. Something must have happened. She hoped Mira was all right, but if the bird *was* caught, they needed another plan. Both to help the bird and to save everyone else. And *soon.* Diana glanced at the demon. Augustus stood listlessly by his side, a fabric bag filled with vials of potions resting at his feet. She swallowed hard. She didn't want to do what she was about to suggest, but it was their only chance.

"I'll be the decoy," said Diana.

"Excuse me?" Sakina said.

"If Mira could do it, so can I."

"Except Mira can *fly,*" Sakina replied.

"You stay hidden in the woods," said Diana. "I'll head to the dock. I'll distract the demon, try to get him away from the runway and onto the dock so he's far from Augustus. When he reaches it, you get to Augustus, grab the ingredients, and put them into the canteen. Be sure to cover your hand to take out the mushroom safely—Augustus said it can be lethal if it touches skin."

"I don't know about this." Sakina shook her head. "What if he traps you at the edge of the dock?"

"I can always swim," Diana said. "And Augustus said the demon arrived on a rowboat. It's probably still anchored at the dock. I can hop on that and row out to sea if I need to—assuming he can't glide over water."

"I don't know." Sakina pursed her lips. "It's not worth the risk. And even if all goes according to plan and I can get to Augustus, how do we know the demon won't turn around and see me? Then what do we do?"

"He won't see you because I'm the one he wants. I'll keep him busy. Trust me, he won't have eyes for anything else."

Sakina studied her friend. And then she said, "I wish I was as brave as you."

"What are you talking about?" Diana said. "You're here, aren't you?"

"I am," she said, "but I'm also terrified. You do what needs doing. You take risks to help people without even thinking about what the consequences could be for you. It's who you are."

"I'm scared, too. I know the consequence and it terrifies me," Diana said gently. "Being scared doesn't make you less brave. I think, in some ways, it makes you even more brave. We can do this," she assured Sakina.

"Ready or not," said Sakina. She stood at the edge of the forest and nodded to Diana.

Silently, stealthily, Diana inched down the tree line, hidden behind the overgrowth, until she had a straight shot to the darkened dock across from where the demon stood on the lit runway.

The demon scanned the landscape. Diana fidgeted. He had to look away eventually. She didn't want to hurry out under his watchful eye. Catching him off guard was critical.

Come on, she murmured. She heard the demon grumble. At last he lifted the bag of potions and turned toward the glittering golden chariot. He glided down the lit runway and shoved the bag of potions inside the vessel.

It was time.

Diana dashed down to the darkened dock. Once she was there, standing midway upon the wooden planks, she cleared her throat and announced, "Let him go!"

The demon startled. He turned. His dark gray eyes landed on hers. A chill passed through Diana.

"Now, this is indeed puzzling. How did you manage to get here all by yourself?" He cocked his head to the side.

"The townspeople are indisposed at this time," Diana said coolly.

"You took out more than a hundred people?" the demon replied, brow arched as he evaluated her. "If so, that's impressive. I can see why he wants you." The demon chuckled. "But do you honestly think you're the first person I have hunted who thinks they can outwit me? Getting out of metal handcuffs is a fine hat trick, but it can only get you so far. The island is surrounded by a solid force field thanks to your friend here, so you cannot escape. Not by boat or by any other means, except with me," he said. "Sooner or later this game of cat and mouse will end, and there can only be one victor. And considering I am immortal, you could say I have all the time in the world."

"I'm not trying to run," Diana said. "I'm here. I came of my own volition."

"You expect me to believe you will accompany me willingly?" He moved off the runway and floated above the water. His hovering form moved closer to her. "As you know very well, I was not born yesterday."

"This is not a game," Diana said. She pushed down the chill from watching him levitate in midair. "I want this over. And I'll only go willingly on one condition: Let my friends go. Don't burn the village."

"Those are two conditions." His eyes narrowed. "Should have taken those blasted petals out while I had the chance. No matter, you're not getting away. That much is certain."

He floated closer. The Lasso of Truth was hooked on his elbow. Diana stood still. It was working. He was coming toward her. He was leaving Augustus behind.

The demon jerked to a stop.

No!

Diana's breath caught. In an instant, the demon reversed course until he'd returned to the runway.

Stalking over to the chariot, the demon grabbed Augustus by the wrist. He yanked the boy forward down the glittering runway. Panic filled Diana's body. This wasn't part of the plan. He wasn't supposed to take Augustus along with him!

Smoke rose off the demon in wisps as he levitated away, crossed the patch of sand, and moved onto the dock where Diana stood. With each movement the demon made forward, Augustus at his side, Diana inched back. The closer he grew, the more she could see how the gray of his eyes swirled like storms.

The demon paused. And then—wordlessly—he burst forward like a sudden gust of powerful wind. Diana ducked as his paper-thin hand shot toward her. His fingers swirled again; he reached for her hair. Diana darted and jumped back, narrowly dodging him.

Turning, Diana took off at a clipped pace until she skidded to a stop at the end of the dock. The demon's rowboat drifted behind her. The ocean crashed against the dock. The demon blocked the path in front of her, the only way back to the shore.

Diana couldn't risk trying to run past the

demon—he'd catch her. She'd need to jump into the ocean and swim away from him. The demon's rowboat had floated a bit farther out, but she could pull the rope and bring it back, or she could run to the chariot and dig through Augustus's bag of potions. Maybe she could use something in there to hold off the demon, at least for a little while.

Suddenly from the corner of her eye, Diana spotted a flash of movement. *Sakina!* She'd emerged from the forest and stood on the sandy shore.

No! Diana wanted to shout. *Not yet!*

In a split second the demon darted forward. He grabbed Diana's wrist. Sparks of pain shot up Diana's arm.

"I believe this is quite literally the end of the road for you." The demon smirked. "Now back to your two conditions. The thing about me you must understand is that I do not entertain such nonsense," he growled.

"I suppose it may be best to cut my losses with the bird," the demon grumbled. "I would have liked to have it, but this has still been a profitable night. The two of you are bounty enough."

Just then a breeze accompanied by a dash of blue swept through the sky. It was Mira! She appeared frazzled, her feathers ruffled, but there she was. Diana nearly shook with relief. Mira fluttered to a smooth boulder on the shore. She settled down upon it and lit her eyes into the dark sea.

"The gamma gazelle?" The demon paused, his eyes focusing on the bird. "It is! Almost as though it were meant to be . . . ," he murmured.

The bird pecked at the rock and sang to herself. Carefully, the demon inched forward. He tugged at Augustus's and Diana's wrists, wrenching them alongside him.

"A gamma gazelle is even more beautiful in person," the demon marveled, stepping onto the shore. "There are only three of them left in all the world." He turned and growled to Augustus, "Stay put. Do not move until I tell you. Understood?"

"Yes, sir," Augustus said blankly.

The demon released Augustus from his grip. With his hand outstretched, he moved carefully toward Mira, dragging Diana along with him.

From the corner of her eye, Diana saw Sakina

emerge from behind a tree. She walked carefully and steadily toward Augustus. Diana tensed. Augustus was no longer right next to the demon, but he was still close. Dangerously close. Diana didn't move a muscle, afraid to make a sound lest she give her friend away.

Diana breathed through the painful sensation of the demon's grip. So far his eyes remained focused on the bird. He seemed to notice nothing but the creature.

"There we go," he muttered. His outstretched fingertips grazed Mira. But before he could grab her, the bird fluttered and flew, landing on another boulder a few steps away.

Diana smiled, filling with hope. The bird was a pro at this.

"Come on already. Only a few more paces," the demon said, inching along behind Mira. "A pity I will have to burn her more by grabbing her. Alas. The feathers should grow back eventually."

Sakina was almost there. Almost next to Augustus. Slowly, Sakina retrieved the canteen tied to her waist belt, and then—

“What was that?” The demon’s back straightened. Quickly, he turned around.

Diana swallowed. It was too late. He’d seen Sakina!

“You all are long past the level of amusement,” he snarled. “I do not know how either of you got out of those chains or where the godforsaken villagers have gone off to, but this stops now. Augustus—grab her and tie her up. There is rope in the chariot. Make sure the bindings are firm so she stays put.”

“Yes, sir,” Augustus said blankly. He stalked toward Sakina.

“Fight him!” Diana shouted.

Sakina didn’t move. She seemed stuck to the spot.

“Sakina, please!” Diana pleaded. “I know you don’t want to battle him. But it’s our only chance.”

They needed the potion—it was the only thing that could save them. They were so close.

“Oh, come now, Diana. Do not be so hard on her. Fear is a natural response in the face of inevitable death,” the demon said. His attention turned back to the bird. “Come along, girl, I have some seeds for you,” he said in a sugary voice. He took a step toward

Mira. "Pumpkin and sesame. Sunflower, too. They are in my chariot—return with me and you shall be given everything you have ever dreamed."

Diana watched Augustus approach Sakina with growing dread. She strained against the demon's scorching grip. Why wasn't Sakina doing anything? Augustus took another leaden step toward her. And then he stopped.

Furtively, he opened his pocket, grabbed a piece of fabric, and gingerly pulled out the flume mushroom. Then he carefully pulled out the icta seed. Sakina shoved the water canteen toward him. Quickly, he stuffed both inside. Sakina tightened the canteen and shook it.

Diana's eyes widened. Augustus glanced at Diana and winked. He'd been pretending this whole time! And they'd mixed up the potion so stealthily that the demon hadn't noticed.

The demon stood with Diana about ten feet away. Sakina couldn't risk running over to them, lest the demon hear her steps and retreat. She saw Sakina's hesitant expression; her friend had thought through the same risk.

But then Diana smiled. Even if Sakina couldn't take a chance running toward them, she could still throw the canteen!

Throw it, she mouthed to Sakina. She nodded to the container.

Sakina looked puzzled for a moment, but then she nodded. With a quick flick of her wrist, she tossed the canteen. Diana watched it spin in the air, her heart pounding in her chest. And there it was. Mere inches from her grasp. Diana shot her hand out and strained against the demon's grip. She caught it!

"Now what?" the demon snarled, jerking back to look at her.

It was now or never.

Diana popped the lid off with her thumb, careful not to drop the container. Before the demon could say anything more, she leaned forward and splashed the potion on him.

Like the bird and the boulder, the liquid went straight through him.

He glanced down at his torso and then at Diana.

"Trying to hydrate me?" He smiled. With a finger,

he flicked the canteen from Diana's hand. It clattered to the ground.

Diana's hopes wavered—they'd gambled on the potion Augustus had whipped up, but the demon looked as powerful as ever. Had it really failed? A botched experiment they would pay for with their lives?

"I must say, I did not take you for being quite this silly. The things children do—"

His smile froze. The sound of sizzling filled the air. Then steam began rising rapidly from his body—no longer compact, his body morphed and expanded around him.

Angry howls tore from him and echoed through the night sky. "What have you done?" he growled. "You stupid, stupid girl!"

His hands flew to his face, releasing Diana. His mouth twisted into an angry slant. He groaned and bent at the waist. His eyes blinked rapidly. He jerked forward and back, as though trying to expel the liquid—but it was too late.

Falling to the ground, the demon writhed and moaned. Diana held her breath. Waiting.

After a few tense moments, the demon rose. Diana jumped back. He lunged at her but then froze in midair before falling to the ground. He groaned as his body began to grow limp.

Vapors rose from his rapidly deflating body like steam emanating from a boiling pot of water.

"Big—mistake—girl," the demon panted. "You have—made him—mad."

"Who?" Diana shouted. "I deserve to know!"

The demon's voice grew quieter. His figure began to fade in and out of focus.

"He . . . always . . . gets . . . what . . . he . . . wants."

More sounds tumbled from his lips, but they were scrambled, garbled as he rapidly evaporated into the night sky. Diana strained her ears to make sense of them, but it was no use. Diana, Augustus, and Sakina stood motionless, watching as the demon grew more and more translucent.

And then he was gone.

Diana let out the breath she'd been holding.

"And *now* the game is over," she said evenly.

"You did it, Diana," Augustus breathed out.

"*We* did it," Diana told them. She leaned down,

picked up the Lasso of Truth from the sandy beach, and tucked it in her belt loop. "We all did it together."

"Way to go, pretending to be enchanted," Diana told Augustus. "You had me completely fooled until you winked at me."

"Same here." Sakina laughed. "I *really* didn't want to battle you."

"My father didn't manage to get all the petals out of my ears." Augustus grinned. "Turns out even a few fragments will do. I decided to take a calculated risk and see if it could work out— Your hand!" he exclaimed at Diana.

Diana glanced down at her wrist. The burn from where the demon had held her stung. Her wrist and palm were scorched red and throbbing. But, looking at Augustus, she could see that his wounds were as severe as her own.

"I know." He nodded and winced. "It still hurts. I can get something for both of us," he said. "It'll be easy enough to whip up a concoction."

Villagers began emerging from the tree line. Their pitchforks and flaming torches were gone. Grass and dirt smudged their clothing. Some limped. For a moment Diana worried—the demon was gone, but did his spell remain?

A woman with ginger hair in a billowing cotton dress approached them. Diana recognized her as Thea, the woman the demon had commanded earlier.

"Augustus," she asked. Her blank expression was now replaced with concern. "Are you all right? What are you doing out here at this hour? What am *I* doing here?"

"Why is the golden chariot set out on the runway?" a man asked. "It can't be there unless Zeus himself is here."

"Was someone going to steal it?"

"My head hurts," another moaned.

"I had the strangest dream."

They glanced at one another and then looked at Sakina and Diana.

"Who are they?"

"What is going on?"

"It's a long story," Augustus said. "Someone evil was here. A demon. He forced us to do awful things.

He was about to have us set our own nation on fire."

The villagers exchanged horrified looks.

"But he's gone," Augustus assured them, "and we're safe now."

"But where did he come from?" someone asked.

"How did he convince us to do his evil work?" asked another.

"I would *never* set my own home on fire. Do you hear me? Never!"

The conversation grew louder as people began speaking over one another.

"I'll explain soon," Augustus promised. "But in the meantime, I have to help . . . my friends." He looked at Sakina and Diana. "Come with me, please. I'll get you all the things you need to return home."

Home.

Diana felt a burst of emotion rise within her. They may have defeated the demon, but the women of Themyscira still needed her help.

Diana looked to the horizon as the sun began to rise in the distance. The sky became streaked with purple and red as the night disappeared and a new day rose over the village. Though the sun brought with it light, all Diana felt was the darkness of despair. Too many worries still crowded her heart. Augustus said he could create an antidote to wake the women, but what if he couldn't? And then there was the other matter—she looked back at the empty golden chariot still resting on the runway and fidgeted remembering the demon's final words: *He always gets what he wants.*

Who was *he*? Was he still going to try to find her?

Chapter Seventeen

The sun shone bright over Sáz now. The room they were clustered inside was tiny—off the apothecary's main store. Diana watched Augustus crush a petal in a mortar and pestle. He twisted a seed from the inside of a berry and inserted it into a glass vial. He was a good potion maker, Diana reminded herself. There was no doubt about it. But it was a brand-new potion for him. . . . She hoped with her whole heart that it would work; the fate of Themyscira rested entirely upon this antidote.

Glancing out the window, Diana saw the bonfire was out at last. People cleaned up charred branches and swept away debris. The sound of children's laughter and the humming of music could be heard through the windows of the tiny space. Was her own homeland as silent as she'd left it? The urgency of returning home ate away at her. She looked down at the clear lotion Augustus had applied to her wrist, where the demon's touch had burned her. To her relief, it was healing.

"I still can't make sense of how you broke out of the handcuffs," Sakina said. She turned to Augustus. "I wish you could've seen it. They were made of solid steel."

"That is fascinating," Augustus said. "Squeezing your hands through the cuffs is conceivable, but tearing them off? That goes against the laws of physics. How *did* you break them?"

"I don't know," Diana said. She herself couldn't believe all the feats she'd managed to accomplish. For the first time she realized that, as much as she didn't know about the world, there was just as much about *herself* she had yet to discover. But one lesson she learned today: she was stronger than she had realized.

Augustus pulled out a pot, filled it with water, and placed it on a burner.

"It's a kind of magic, what you do," said Diana. "Seeing something that doesn't exist and imagining it into being."

"Thanks. Maybe one day my father will agree with you, too."

Diana thought of her mother and their endless circular arguments about her training. Thinking of her mother now, trapped in an eternal sleep, made her ache. She'd give just about anything to wake her.

The back door creaked open.

"I'm almost done, Mr. Broderick," Augustus said. "I mixed the powder first, like you said. It should only be a few more minutes under the heat and then it needs to cool."

But it wasn't Mr. Broderick. The person who stepped inside was Brutus—Augustus's father.

"Thought I'd find you here," the man said. He shut the door behind him.

"Y-you know about my space for potion making?" The boy stared at his father.

"Of course I do," he said. "You've been coming here since you were about eight, haven't you?"

"Y-yes." Augustus blushed.

Brutus turned to the two girls.

"I came to apologize to you. All of you," he said. His eyes were fixed on the floor. "I can't begin to tell you how sorry I am. I don't understand how I could have been so ready to hand over my own son."

"It wasn't you, Father," Augustus said quickly. "Everyone was under his spell."

"A part of me was locked away," Brutus said, "telling me my actions were wrong, but I couldn't access my free will. His words *felt* so right. I should have fought it. I could have tried harder."

"We're okay now, Father." Augustus hurried to Brutus and hugged him.

"Augustus invented a potion. It destroyed the demon," Diana said. "He came up with it on the spot, all by himself."

"Is that true, son?" Brutus looked at Augustus in wonder.

"It wasn't too difficult," the boy said bashfully.

"Once I thought harder about his composition, I worked backward to discover how those properties could be easily disrupted."

"You saved this town," his father said.

"Not alone." Augustus smiled at Sakina and Diana. "We were a team. But yes, I helped. The potion was an important part of taking him down."

Augustus's father studied the boy quietly.

"I've always been afraid of your potion making desires," he said. "Don't understand the first thing about how it works. But maybe I should be less afraid and more open to you following your dreams."

"Are you saying . . . ?" Augustus's voice trailed off.

"You can do both, can't you?" his father said. "Help me with chariots *and* study potion-making with Mr. Broderick?"

"I already do," Augustus said shyly.

"Maybe you can teach me a thing or two."

Brutus leaned down and embraced his son. Diana smiled with pride for Augustus just as the clear liquid in the vial turned a sunflower yellow.

"It's ready," Augustus said. He stepped away from

Brutus, placed a sprig of mint inside the vial, and screwed a misting-spray top onto it before handing it to Diana. "Shake it and spray inside and outside the palace. Everyone asleep on Themyscira will be awake within moments."

"Is the force field around Sáz gone?" Sakina asked.

"It was as soon as the demon was destroyed," Augustus said. "You're free to go home anytime."

They left the shop and walked toward the dock. Turning down the main street, people burst out of their homes, hurrying toward them.

"How long were you going to stay cooped up in Broderick's shop?" a woman huffed.

"You knew I was there?" Augustus said.

"It's a small town," a young girl giggled. She took a step forward and clasped her hands. "I can't believe I got to meet real live heroes. My friends won't believe it."

Heroes? Diana chuckled. But it was true, wasn't it? The three of them had been brave—and they had saved the day.

"Thank you," a woman said. She approached the

trio and handed the girls a basket of fresh blueberry muffins.

"This town owes you an enormous debt," said a man. It was Marco.

"You shouldn't have had to save us," an older gentleman said sadly. "You're children."

"Don't understand how a thing like this happens," another said, shaking his head.

"We'll be sending a message to the gods to let them know what happened," said another. "They will not be happy when they find out."

The townspeople walked the girls to the first plane. They stood at the edge of the woods and waved.

"I wish you could stay a bit longer," Augustus said wistfully as they neared the chariot. "Now that everything is safe again, we could actually have some fun. There's a cave not far from the shore with the most beautiful stingrays. . . ."

"The sooner we get home, the better," Diana said, worried about her mother and the others who were still motionless on Themyscira. She glanced around the island. Everything *seemed* idyllic now, but whoever *he* was who had commissioned the demon to capture her was still out there. The quicker they could reach home, the better.

A cream-colored chariot awaited them on the runway.

"How will we get this back to you?" Diana asked, gesturing to the chariot.

"It's yours," said Augustus, waving a hand at the transport.

"Augustus, it's beautiful! But it must cost a fortune."

"Well, what's the going rate for saving an entire town?" Augustus asked with a laugh. "I helped make this one myself, apprenticing with my father last month. I would be honored if you would take it with you to get home."

"Thank you," said Diana, bowing her head.

"Maybe one day you can use it to come visit." He handed her a bag. "There's enough powder in here for many flights."

"Not 'maybe'! Definitely," Sakina told him.

Diana smiled and nodded.

The three embraced, and then Diana and Sakina hopped into the chariot. Mira grabbed the lead rope and lifted it with her beak. They sprinkled the powder and waited—within seconds the powder was absorbed and the chariot lifted into the air. Augustus jumped and waved as the chariot rose higher and higher. Soon the palm trees, the sandy shores, the cliffs, and the lava river along the middle of Sáz grew smaller and smaller until the island completely disappeared from view.

Diana held up the glass vial. It was still yellow, and its consistency was the same as it had been when they'd left. She wanted to trust it would work, but her optimism cracked a bit. An eternal sleep meant *forever.*

"I'm worried, too," Sakina said, watching Diana's pinched expression.

"It'll work." Diana swallowed.

It has to.

Chapter Eighteen

Diana stood straighter as Themyscira came into full view. The sun shone bright above them, on the cloudless day. There they were, the jagged cliff-lined shores, her favorite olive tree jutting over the sea, the stone temples, and the cream-colored palace—her home. She felt a rush of relief at seeing the familiar rosebushes and gardens.

The chariot touched down on the shore, and they hurried past the empty white tents and bare tables still set up for the Chará festival. Heaviness settled over Diana. The tents should have been filled with people today, laughter and conversation flowing everywhere she turned. There should have been women practicing combat moves and trying out different weapons in the coliseum. Her mother, along with other leaders, should have been huddled close in deep conversation.

But the island was silent.

The girls parted the palace doors. They stepped onto the marble tiles and rushed down the hall, straight to the guest quarters. Diana put a hand to her mouth when they stepped inside. The scent of oranges was gone, but the scene remained, the same as the night before. All the women were exactly as they had been: asleep.

"Well, here goes nothing," she said. She picked up the glass misting bottle and sprayed the perimeter of the hall. Unlike the citrus smell of the original potion, this one had no discernible scent save for a hint of mint. Diana traversed the hallways, misting the potion, and in every room she passed she found at least one sleeping woman.

Joining Sakina in the main hall, they watched the women. And waited.

"It'll work," Sakina said. "Right?"

Diana bit her lip.

She weaved through the women sleeping on the

floor until she reached her mother. Diana kneeled down to watch Queen Hippolyta's sleeping form move almost imperceptibly with each breath.

"Any sign of *your* mother coming to?" Diana asked Sakina.

Sakina crouched by the velvet sofas, next to her mother, Queen Khadijah. She swallowed and shook her head.

A few more heart-pounding moments passed. Diana shivered. Augustus was a good potion maker, this much she knew—but what if this potion was the one that failed?

But then her mother yawned.

Another woman coughed.

Others began to rouse.

"I shut my eyes for two seconds," a woman grumbled. "How is it already daylight?"

"I nodded off with my wine goblet still full?" another woman said in disbelief, staring at the cup in her hand.

"You fell asleep, too?" someone asked.

Suddenly Queen Khadijah woke with a start.

"Mother!" Sakina cried, reaching over to give her mother a hug.

"Such a greeting!" Her mother rubbed her eyes, returning her daughter's embrace. "What did I do to merit such a warm hug?"

"Wait. Did *everyone* fall asleep? How?"

Voices began to overlap one another.

"I'd like to know the same thing," Queen Hippolyta said. She rose from her chaise longue.

"Mother!" Diana's voice rose. She turned toward her mother.

The queen placed a hand on her hip. Concern etched her face.

"How *did* all of us fall asleep at the same time?"

"It was an enchantment," said Diana. "A potion put you to sleep late last night while you were relaxing in this hall. Something called the misting potion of eternal sleep. But we managed to get the antidote."

"A mist of eternal sleep? But security during the festival is so tight! How did something like this happen?" Queen Hippolyta asked incredulously.

As best they could, Diana and Sakina explained the events of the previous night to everyone. The boy who'd followed the Scholars' ship to the island. The land of Sáz. The demon.

Everyone listened in silence. When the girls finished, Diana's mother took her daughter's hand in her own and squeezed it.

"Diana," she said. "You mean to tell me the two of you slipped off to another land by yourselves?"

"Mira came with us," Sakina interjected. "We couldn't have done it without her."

"We had no choice, Mother," Diana told her. "Everyone was asleep. Nothing I could do roused you. The only chance to wake you was to go with the boy and get the antidote."

"And the boy, Diana?" her mother asked. "Did you also not have an opportunity to tell me about him?"

"I did know about the boy." Diana swallowed. "I could have told you but I wasn't sure what would happen. He looked so scared and seemed so helpless. I know boys aren't allowed on our island. I wasn't sure what to do, and then, well, everyone fell asleep."

"I wish you'd told me," her mother said. "Males aren't allowed here, this much is true. But you need to have faith in us that we would do the right thing. This was a very serious situation; I should have been apprised of it."

"You're right, Mother. I'm sorry."

"I'm glad you helped protect his people," her mother said. "Still, it's not news any mother wants to hear. We want to protect our children."

"But it worked out. We were able to protect ourselves."

Her mother looked at her for a long moment. She wore an expression Diana did not recognize.

"You absolutely did," she finally said. Her gaze shifted to Diana's belt. "And I see you had a lasso for good luck."

"Oh. Sorry." She blushed, handing it to the queen. "But there is something else." Diana hesitated. "Something strange happened on the island."

"What do you mean?"

"I don't know how to explain it, except I did things I've never done before."

"I was there." Sakina leaned in. "You should have

seen her, Your Majesty. She scaled a cliff as flat and smooth as a wall. It stretched up hundreds of feet. She fought off armed men. She broke us out of metal cuffs with her bare hands. Metal cuffs! She was amazing."

"Excuse me. Who figured out what we were up against in the first place?" Diana bumped Sakina's shoulder.

"Fine." Sakina nodded. "I guess we were *both* pretty fantastic."

"Yes, we were." Diana smiled.

"Is that true?" Queen Hippolyta asked Diana. "You broke out of metal handcuffs?"

There was a gentle, faint rumbling in the distance. No one else seemed to notice. Diana frowned. Was she so exhausted that she was hearing things?

"I have no idea how it happened, but I did." Diana nodded. "I was so angry. It seemed like the demon was going to win after all, and I don't know. . . . Something shifted in me, and I did it. I can't make any sense of *how,* just that it happened."

Her mother hesitated, but before she could

speak, the island trembled again—harder this time. Women gasped and steadied themselves on chairs and the wall. Diana gripped the edge of the window. Picture frames and vases trembled.

"Feels like an earthquake," said Queen Khadijah, her expression pale.

"We don't get earthquakes here," Queen Hippolyta said. She quickly turned to the Amazon warriors. "Weapons out. On the grounds, now!"

Wordlessly, everyone rushed to the palace grounds with weapons drawn. The earth had stopped moving. Glancing around, Diana saw nothing amiss; the land looked the same as it ever had.

"Let's divide and search," Queen Hippolyta began. "Antiope, you take the—"

"Binti?" Diana squinted into the distance.

The wolf had appeared over a hill.

"Look!" Sakina pointed. "Arya's with her, too."

Both animals hurried over the hillside together. Diana drew a sharp intake of breath as they drew near. Each carried a person, limp, across their backs.

No. Diana recoiled. She willed it not to be true—

but there was no denying the red masks and gold armor. Cylinda and Yen. They'd left for their shift to guard Doom's Doorway yesterday. If they were here, that meant the door was unguarded. Diana had no idea what the consequences of leaving the door unattended would be.

Diana and Sakina broke into a run, the other women not far behind. Binti and Arya gingerly let the women down to the ground. Neither of them moved. Diana's mother bent down and removed Yen's mask. Her face was cut, her left eye bloody and swollen shut. Cylinda's face was bruised, too, and her arm was twisted at a strange angle. The women were awake, but just barely.

"It opened," Yen croaked.

"The door?" Queen Hippolyta stared at Yen.

"A crack. Just a crack."

The blood drained from Aunt Antiope's face. "A crack? Are you certain?"

Yen nodded weakly.

"We need to go! Now!" Aunt Antiope cried out. Immediately a team of Amazon warriors raced toward the hillside to Doom's Doorway. Diana moved to follow them, but her mother rested a hand on her shoulder, gentle yet firm.

Diana watched them shrink into the distance, trepidation filling her heart.

"Did you hear anything before the door opened?" Queen Hippolyta asked. "Conversation?"

"Things are not right," Yen murmured. And then she fainted.

Queen Hippolyta kneeled and scooped Yen into her arms. Another warrior lifted Cylinda and draped her over her shoulder.

"Back to the palace," Queen Hippolyta shouted resolutely. "Now!"

Chapter Nineteen

Two twin beds were hastily set up in a palace suite. Marcela, a healer, pressed a warm compress against Cylinda's arm. A medicinal paste was applied along Yen's face and arms.

"Thank you for your service," Queen Hippolyta told the woman. "We are lucky we have the best in their fields on a day like today."

"My pleasure," Marcela said. "The injuries appear worse than they are. They'll be well again in no time."

The earth hadn't quaked again, but the memory still vibrated through Diana's body. She looked at Cylinda and Yen. Outside of their usual armor, with plain white blankets draped over them, they looked hardly older than Diana herself. She hoped Marcela was right and that they'd be back to normal in no time.

"There's no need for all this fuss over a few scrapes and bruises," Yen said. She moved to sit up and then grimaced. "What's happening? I can't open my left eye."

"Now lay your head back down," Marcela instructed. "The injuries you sustained aren't permanent, but they're still serious. The cream needs time to work. Your eye will heal faster the more you rest and let the medicine do what it needs to do.

"Looks like you broke your arm," Marcela told Cylinda. "Just a hairline break, though. A few weeks in a sling and it should set, so long as you don't use it much and get as much rest as possible."

"They'll remain in the palace with us," Queen Hippolyta said. "We'll make sure they're well cared for."

"Thank you," Cylinda said softly.

"Eat one of these berries three times a day," Marcela instructed Yen. "And then rub this paste over your eye for the next few weeks. I know it hurts, but this will pass, and soon enough you won't even remember it happened."

"Impossible," Yen murmured. "I won't forget for as long as I live."

"What happened?" Diana asked delicately.

"Yes," Queen Hippolyta said. "Anything you can tell us would be helpful."

"Nothing seemed out of the ordinary at first," Yen said. "Hours passed with not so much as a sound. But then there were noises through the night."

"What sorts of noises?" the queen asked.

"Conversations—quite heated. We didn't think much of it at first," Yen explained. "The Underworld isn't known for its silence, and Hades isn't exactly the most even-tempered of gods."

"But then this morning we heard a loud noise," Cylinda said. "I thought it was a howl at first. Assumed one of the wolves on the island was playing around. But soon after, the door began to shake."

"The door? It was *shaking*?" the queen repeated. "Are you certain?"

"Yes." Cylinda nodded. "It sounded like something was trying to break it down from the inside."

"We followed the protocol you taught us," Yen said. "We blockaded the door. We hammered in the stop-gap nails. Whatever was behind it grew angrier. It pushed and shoved so hard that the ground beneath us began to shake."

"Not just beneath you," Diana said. "It shook the entire island."

"It was intense." Yen shuddered. "Even with the stop-gap nails and the blockade, whatever it was managed to crack the door open. Not more than a few inches, though. Nothing more."

"The shaking from the earth dislodged rocks from the hillside," Cylinda said. "We had an avalanche. We couldn't get out of the way before we got caught up in it, but it could have been worse. Thank goodness the snow leopard and Binti heard us calling out for help."

"The door is covered with rocks?" the queen asked.

"Yes," Cylinda said. "Whatever is trying to get out definitely can't now."

"Nothing's ever tried to get out of there before,"

Diana said slowly. "At least, not as long as I've been alive."

Queen Hippolyta nodded. Worry clouded her face.

"We are sorry." Cylinda looked down at her lap. "We volunteered to help this week. We hate that we let you down."

"Let us down? Nonsense," the queen told them. "We'll triple the guards at the door as a precaution until we can figure out what's going on, but for now both of you have only one mission: to rest and get better."

Diana wandered into her bedroom. Sakina lay on her bed, a pillow propped under her head, looking out the window.

"Have you finished talking to your mother?" Diana asked, settling down next to her.

"For now," Sakina said. "I don't think we'll be done discussing what happened for a long time."

"You're probably right."

"My time with you is always memorable, but I'm pretty sure this week will stand out for years to come," Sakina said. "If you weren't here to confirm it, I'd have thought I made it all up."

"Same here. I can't believe how much happened in just twelve hours. Feels like twelve days have passed." Diana smiled at her friend. "And, Sakina . . . thank you. You didn't have to stand up for me and go there with me."

"Excuse me." Sakina raised her eyebrows. "That's what best friends do, isn't it? And you have to admit, we make a pretty good team, don't we?"

"The absolute best," Diana said. She hugged her friend.

A quick knock on the door interrupted them.

"Diana?" Queen Hippolyta stood in the hallway. "Sorry to interrupt you girls. But if I can have a quick word with you, Diana?"

"See what I mean?" Sakina smiled at Diana.

"Walk with me," Diana's mother said. They stepped outside the palace and onto the grounds. The tents were filling with commotion. Women were setting out their wares. The land hummed with joy. The festival was, at long last, officially beginning.

"Sáz. They build chariots for the gods, don't they?" her mother asked.

"Yes." Diana nodded.

"It's strange that a demon would choose to go and cause mayhem on a protected land, of all places."

"We were trying to figure out the same thing. But he said . . ." Diana hesitated. This was the part she hadn't told her mother earlier. She hadn't wanted to worry her.

"Diana," her mother said gently. "Whatever it is, even if it's bad, I need to know. It's the only way to figure this out."

"The demon . . . he said he was there to capture me for someone. A *he*."

"He?" A troubled look crossed her mother's face.

"This whole mission. The boy's arrival. The demon enchanting the village. It was all about getting me to someone I only heard referred to as *he*. But I never found out who *he* is or why he wanted me in the first place."

"Did the demon say whether or not the *he* was a god or a person or some other entity?" Queen Hippolyta asked.

"No." Diana shook her head. "But not a god. I don't think so. The demon planned to burn the lands to the ground to make sure the gods didn't learn what he'd done."

"I see," her mother said. "And the demon is gone? You're certain of it?"

"Yes. We watched him disappear. But what if whoever tasked him to get me sends more demons after me? He seems like he won't go down without a fight."

"He—whoever *he* is—won't get to you here," her mother said. "The island is safe and protected. But until we can figure out what is going on, we will assign extra monitoring and guard shifts."

"Good idea," Diana said.

"But, Diana." Queen Hippolyta looked down at her daughter. "You were something else, weren't you?"

"I guess watching all the women over the years seeped into me," Diana said. "I don't know how, but I managed to do what was needed."

"It's because you are the kind of person who will move mountains for others. You have a hero's heart, and you'll do whatever is necessary to push yourself as far as you can to help those who need you most." She placed a hand on her daughter's shoulder. "And I think it's time to talk about your training."

For a moment, Diana thought she misunderstood what her mother had said. But then she looked up at the queen.

"My training?" Diana repeated.

"Yes." Queen Hippolyta nodded.

"You think I can do it?" she asked. "I know you might not think I'm a natural, but I've picked up so much. More than I even realized."

"You've always been a natural. You possess a greatness that doesn't come around often. It's what I planned to discuss with you after the festival concluded. But the thing about greatness is that it comes with a heavy responsibility. I've worried you are too young to take on so much. But I'm beginning to see I was wrong. You have a strong sense of justice; it runs deep in your veins. I cannot expect you to stand to the side when injustice arises."

"You will let me learn to fight?" Diana asked slowly.

"I will see to your training myself," her mother said. "Your aunt will be pleased. She's been after me for months."

"She was right, huh?" Diana grinned.

"I can own my mistakes." Her mother laughed.

"Thank you so much, Mother." Diana leapt up and hugged her tightly. "I can't wait to be a true warrior."

"You already are, Diana." Her mother returned the embrace.

They walked back toward the tents. Music sounded through the island as the festival celebrations picked up once more.

Diana searched the crowd until she saw her friend. Sakina stood by a stall of flowing dresses, close to the coliseum.

"It happened, didn't it?" Sakina said once Diana approached her, noting the look of elation on Diana's face. "Your mom said you can train?"

"Yep." Diana laughed. "She said yes."

"I knew it!" Sakina gave Diana a high five. "You're going to be the most amazing warrior the world has ever seen. I am never wrong about my predictions."

A bell sounded in the distance.

"A class is about to begin!" Sakina's eyes lit up.

"What kind of class?" Diana asked.

"No idea." Sakina shrugged. "Doesn't matter. It'll be fun because . . ."

"We'll be doing it together," Diana finished.

"Exactly!" Sakina grinned. "Ready?"

"Ready or not, here I come!"

Just a short while ago, Diana had been afraid that life as she knew it was over—her island had been in danger, and she had no one to turn to for help or guidance. But now, after everything they had gone through, life *was* different. Now it was full of promise—a promise that things would be even better.

Diana hurried with her best friend toward the palace. Five full days of the festival remained, and she couldn't wait to see everything the week would bring.

Acknowledgments

Thank you so much to my incredible editorial team: Chelsea Eberly, Sasha Henriques, and Sara E. Sargent. Thank you also to Benjamin Harper at Warner Bros. for your insights and wisdom. Many thanks to Alessia Trunfio for the cover art, and to the designer, Tanya Mauler. A huge thank-you to everyone at Random House, DC, and Warner Bros.—it takes a village to create a book. Thank you also to Taylor Martindale Kean and the Full Circle Literary family. Cylinda Parga, Yen M. Tang, Ayesha Mattu, Tracy Lopez, and Becky Albertalli—thank you for your support and friendship. And last but never least: to my three boys and my husband, thank you for lighting my life with your presence.

About the Author

Aisha Saeed is a *New York Times* bestselling author. Her books include the young adult novels *Written in the Stars* and *Yes No Maybe So* (coauthored with Becky Albertalli), the middle-grade novels *Amal Unbound* and *Aladdin: Far from Agrabah,* and the picture book *Bilal Cooks Daal* (illustrated by Anoosha Syed). Aisha is also a founding member of the nonprofit We Need Diverse Books. She lives in Atlanta with her husband and sons.

aishasaeed.com

The sun shone brightly upon the beaches of Themyscira, the golden glow shimmering as though Zeus himself had struck the island with a lightning bolt. Diana stood to the side of the dock, arms crossed, watching women from the Scholar community trudge up the plank toward their ship, lugging bronze, copper, and silver trunks behind them. Just across from Diana stood the sea captain, who unfurled her map and scrutinized the coordinates that would lead them—and Diana's best friend, Sakina—back to their home.

Diana swallowed. Just one week earlier, this very ship had unspooled its anchor into the sea alongside other vessels belonging to women from communities around the world: expert strategists, welders, artists, educators, even fellow warriors from distant lands. They'd descended from abroad to celebrate their cultures and share knowledge with one another at the annual Chará festival. During the day, they'd taught and attended classes ranging from pottery to painting to combat. Each evening, they'd laughed and chatted over lavish feasts, goblets of wine, and the steady hum of music and dancing. At night, Diana and Sakina had taken the Sky Kangas from the royal stables and soared over the island, beyond the looming statues of Aphrodite and Hera and Athena just outside the coliseum walls. They'd plucked the juiciest oranges they could find from Themyscira's groves and then eaten the sweet fruit while standing on the island's cliff-lined shores. Last night the girls had climbed onto the palace's rooftop to gaze at the stars twinkling overhead. It had been the perfect ending to a dramatic week.

The festival had started off bumpy—to put it mildly—but matters had improved since Diana's near-death adventure, which involved an escape from the island of Sáz and a demon who had wished to capture her. She'd not only saved an entire nation on the brink of destruction and woken the Amazons from an endless sleep but also finally convinced her mother to let her train as a warrior. So much had happened, but somehow it had gone by all too quickly.

"Finally!" a voice exclaimed.

Sakina was wheeling a steel trunk as she walked toward Diana. She wore a velvet tunic and gold leggings. Her long dark hair was tucked back in a twist.

"All packed, huh?" Diana said.

"Yep." Sakina set the trunk at her feet. "It was way harder to stuff all my things back in. I had to jump on the trunk to make it shut!"

"Maybe because you picked up so many goodies along the way," Diana teased. "I think—"

Suddenly Diana froze. She squinted as a flash of *something* burst beyond the woods leading toward her palace home. *What was that?* Diana wondered. She scanned the horizon, her heart beating quickly.

It's nothing, she told herself. *You're spooked these*

days, that's all. After what she'd been through, how could she not be?

But then the trees rustled in the distance, the branches shaking violently.

"Diana, what's wrong?" Sakina asked.

Diana didn't reply. Her eyes remained fixed on the swaying tree line. Leaves fluttered to the ground. Diana slid her hand to the sword at her waist. The demon had said someone was hunting for her—and that "he" would find her. *Is this it?* she wondered. *Is he here?* Diana took one careful step forward. Then another. And then—

Arya!

Sakina's snow leopard leapt down from a branch and nimbly planted herself on the ground. Binti, Diana's wolf friend, emerged from the forest and ran into the clearing, playfully chasing the large cat. A rush of relief flooded through Diana. She loosened her hand from the sword's hilt and unclenched her jaw. Everything was fine. The animals were friends. They were simply saying goodbye. Diana was safe.

"He's not here," Sakina said gently. She rested a hand on Diana's arm.

"Right. Of course not," Diana said. She shrugged unconvincingly. "Arya just caught me off guard, that's all."

"That's why you sleep with a dagger under your pillow like it's your security blanket?" Sakina raised her eyebrows. "It's not exactly snuggly."

Diana blushed. She hadn't realized that Sakina had noticed.

"Fine, maybe it's on my mind a little bit," she admitted.

"I get it." Sakina nodded. "I'm ninety-nine percent sure the demon was making it all up, but I still can't help looking over my shoulder now and then."

The knot of tension in the pit of Diana's stomach eased. If anyone would understand, it would be Sakina. They'd gone through the harrowing ordeal that kicked off the Chará festival together. A boy, Augustus, who hailed from the Sáz nation of chariot makers, had found his way to Themyscira, though his presence was forbidden. A gifted potion maker, he'd enchanted the women on the island—guests and warriors alike—into an endless sleep and then begged Diana and Sakina to help him save his people from an evil demon. The demon had hypnotized Augustus's people and threatened to burn their nation to the ground, all so he could capture Diana for a bounty set by a mysterious "him." It had been the most terrifying ordeal of Diana's life—but the three of them had made it through. They'd survived booby traps and lava rivers and violent, hypnotized villagers, and together, they destroyed the demon. But what he'd said in his final moments wouldn't leave her: *He always gets what he wants.*

The words echoed through her mind. They haunted her dreams.

"Nothing's happened," Sakina said, as though reading Diana's thoughts. "The women were woken up by the antidote, and the rest of the week was incident-free."

"But Doom's Doorway . . . ," Diana added, hesitating. "It shook like an earthquake when we returned. That can't have been a coincidence."

"Even if it wasn't," Sakina said, "nothing happened, right? The door didn't open all the way, and the rocks that fell from all the shaking sealed it shut from the outside. And look around—it's not like the guards are taking any chances, are they?" Sakina gestured to the warrior women stationed along the island's edge. The guard posts were often empty in times of peace, but each one was occupied today. The ladies wore white tunics and golden sandals that wrapped to their knees. More than twenty of them stood guard at designated posts around the island.

"Hey." Sakina nudged Diana with her elbow. "If you had your pick of anyone to have your back, it would be the Amazons, wouldn't it?"

"For sure." Diana's shoulders relaxed. Without the specific coordinates, her nation was, by design, untraceable. And even if someone managed to get around that, no one stood a chance against the women of her kingdom—of that much Diana was certain.

"So." She turned to Sakina. "What was your favorite part of the week?"

"You mean other than saving a nation from the brink of destruction?" Sakina laughed. "Kind of hard to top that." She thought for a moment. "I'd say welding was definitely my favorite class. Look at these wheels I added to my trunk!"

"I liked the workshop where we tried out rare weapons," Diana said.

"Wow, shocker," Sakina replied, rolling her eyes good-naturedly.

"It's true, though. Can you believe they let us actually hold the Rinuni sword? It's over two thousand years old."

"That was cool," Sakina agreed.

"And then, well, hanging out with you for a weeklong slumber party. That was pretty great," Diana said.

"I am awesome company, aren't I?" Sakina grinned.

A fluttering in the corner of Diana's eye caught her attention. The Scholar's flag—embroidered with a quill and a scroll—had been unfurled and now flapped in the afternoon breeze.

"I'm going to miss you." Diana's smile faded.

"Me too," Sakina said. "A once-a-year visit with your best friend just isn't enough."

"Mira's great about whisking letters back and forth the rest of the time, but it's not—"

"—the same." Sakina shook her head. "No way."

"Yeah," Diana said. "But at least you have friends back home."

"What do you mean?" Sakina said. "You have friends. What about Cylinda and Yen?"

She pointed to two women in the distance. Cylinda still had a cast on her arm from when she'd guarded Doom's Doorway. The door had shaken the earth violently and caused rocks to fall onto the warriors stationed for duty. Yen still had a patch over her bruised eye.

"Of course," Diana said. "They're great." She adored the women of her land—every last one. "It's just that when you're the only kid on the entire island, it can get a bit lonely."

"Come visit me this year!" Sakina said suddenly. "It's about time."

"Yeah." Diana laughed softly. It wouldn't be the first time she'd try to convince her mother to let her visit her best friend. "Pretty sure we know how that request will go over with my mother. . . ."

"It's simple. Take a Sky Kanga. If they can fly

into the stratosphere and launch into space, they can definitely get you to my place in no time. Our lands aren't even that far apart."

"You know how overprotective she is. She's never been keen on my leaving the island," Diana said.

"But you did leave. Earlier this week," Sakina pointed out. "And visiting me won't involve burning bridges and lava and scary demons."

That was true. Diana had proved she could handle herself, hadn't she? Hope flickered within her.

"Sakina!" a voice interrupted. Queen Khadijah—Sakina's mother—approached them from the docks. She wore a flowing jade-green gown, and her hair was wrapped in a cream scarf pinned with jewels. "Ready to get going? Once we get this trunk on board, we'll be all packed."

"I can help you carry it to the ship, Sakina," Diana offered. "The dock is super bumpy; anything fragile could break."

"Thanks. I should probably put my sword away, too—oh!" Sakina glanced down at her waist. "My sword! I left it on the nightstand next to my bed."

“Be quick,” her mother said. “The wind is favorable and the seas are calm, so it’s best to get going soon.”

Diana and Sakina hurried toward the palace. They walked past the white tents that had shaded the merchant stalls all week. Those tents were now being pulled down and folded into squares, which would be tucked into waiting storage trunks. They wouldn’t see the light of day until the next festival, a year from now.

“I know how I’ll convince my mother,” Diana said as they jogged. “You learned so many awesome combat moves during Aunt Antiope’s training lessons, but you have to keep practicing, don’t you?”

“That’s true.” Sakina brightened. “And who better to learn from than Princess Diana?”

“Can’t argue with you there!” a voice called out.

Antiope! Diana slowed her gait as her aunt approached them.

“Though, I admit, convincing my sister will be a task far more complicated than any combat move.”

“Maybe you can help us?” Diana asked.

“I can try.” She smiled. “Diana, dear, a quick word?”

"I'll grab my sword while you chat," Sakina said. "Be back in a second."

Sakina opened the golden palace doors and slipped inside. Diana turned to her aunt. Blond tendrils framed Antiope's face as she studied Diana carefully.

"Are you all right?" her aunt asked, concern apparent in her green eyes. "With everything that's happened, we haven't had a chance to speak much."

"I'm fine," Diana said quickly. Her mother had only this week allowed Diana to begin her combat training. She didn't want it sidetracked for any reason. "Why wouldn't I be?"

"Oh, I don't know." Antiope laughed a little. "You had a lot going on this week. And, well, I saw you earlier, when the animals were playing in the woods. You were so tense—your shoulders were hunched by your ears."

"Oh." Diana flushed. She hadn't realized she was being watched. "That. Well, I just . . . thought I saw something . . . which I did . . . but . . ."

"It's normal," her aunt said. "You've been through so much. When something traumatic occurs, it takes time to move past it. Just re[illegible]

safe here."

Diana bit her lip. She wanted to [illegible] accept her aunt's assurance and let it go. But—

"Doom's Doorway opened," Diana said. "I know it was just a crack. But that's never happened before. What if something got out?"

"We've inspected every inch of this land," her aunt told her. "And you can see for yourself that we are still on high alert, constantly guarding the island to make absolutely sure. Truly, all is well. But . . ." She tilted her head and searched Diana's expression. "In the meantime, would it help you feel better if we did some training later today?"

"Really?" Diana's eyes shot up toward her aunt's. "I would love that! Can we do the kita hold? And then I wanted to see how to get out of a double crossover switch. Serene looks like she does it without blinking."

"Easy there." Antiope laughed, holding up her hands. "Serene does it so effortlessly because she puts hours of practice into it. To be a true warrior isn't for the faint of heart, and as exciting as it may seem from afar, it is going to be grueling and even a bit dull at times."

"It could never be boring to me," Diana said emphatically. "Can we start once Sakina leaves? It might take my mind off things and help me feel not quite as nervous."

"So it shall be, then." Her aunt nodded. "How about you and I head to the coliseum after cleanup?"

"Thank you." Diana hugged her aunt tightly. With Sakina leaving, this was what she needed: something to look forward to. She rushed into the palace. She couldn't wait to tell her friend.

"Sakina!" Diana called out. She took the marble steps two at a time to the second floor, toward her bedroom. "Guess what Aunt Antiope and I are planning to . . ."

Stepping through the bedroom's open doorway, her voice trailed off. The mahogany bookcase next to the window was overturned. Books were splayed across the floor. Her plush white rug was askew. Necklaces, bracelets, and belts had fallen from their hooks along the wall and were strewn across the ground. Diana tensed. *Sakina!* Where was she?

Glancing at the nightstand, Diana saw: Sakina's sword was gone.

Just then, the door creaked behind her.

"Sakina," Diana said with a rush of relief. "I was getting worried. Were you battling the books or something? Because—"

As Diana turned and faced the door, she felt the blood drain from her face.

It was not Sakina.

Instead a cloaked being stood just inside the doorway.

Silently, it watched her.

Before Diana could move a muscle, before she could say a word, the intruder made a sharp movement, and the door slammed shut.

Heart pounding, Diana stared at the cloaked figure. *This isn't happening. It can't be. Every post around this island is guarded.*

And yet there it was. Watching her. Its head, arms, and hands were shrouded beneath a bulky sage-green cloak. It stood at her height. The scent of roses clung thick and sickeningly sweet in the air. And though she could not see its eyes, she could feel them boring into her.

Cold, raw fear coursed through Diana's body.

What was this thing? Was it sent here to take her to *him*?

Or was this . . . *him*?

“Where is Sakina?” Diana asked in a low voice. “Where’s my friend?”

The intruder tilted its head. It said nothing. Diana shivered. She didn’t know what it was, but she was as certain as she was of her own name that it meant her harm. Diana inched her hand to the sword secured at her belt. *A choke hold,* she thought. *I’ll battle it to the wall, and once it’s cornered, I’ll grab it by its cloak and get some answers.* Carefully she grazed her hand against the emerald-encrusted hilt of her sword. But before she could grasp it, the figure lunged.

Diana deftly leapt out of its way. It swiveled and pounced again. Diana ducked, missing its cloaked grasp by a hairsbreadth. The figure didn’t so much run as it practically flew.

“Help!” she shouted at the top of her lungs. “There’s someone here! In my room! It’s an emergency! Please hurry!”

But no footsteps sounded upon the stairs. The windows in her room were firmly shut. No one could hear her cries for help.

Diana raced for the door. In an instant the creature blocked her path.

Diana fumed. How dare this thing try to attack her in her own home! Drawing her sword, she rushed toward her bed and leapt onto it.

"Stand back," she warned, pointing her blade at the cloaked figure. "I don't want to hurt you. But I won't hesitate."

The assailant stood still, watching her silently. Then it dove again. Diana angled her sword and attacked square at its midsection. But then her stomach dropped. Though the sword had speared straight through the fabric cloak, it was as if she'd sliced thin air. And it certainly *felt* like it—nothing seemed to keep the weaponry in place besides the fabric. The being calmly glanced down at the sword and back at her.

Diana tugged at the weapon, but it was stuck within the fabric. With a cloaked arm, the intruder yanked the sword from its body with such force that Diana lost her grip. Her attacker tossed the blade away, and the weapon skidded beneath Diana's bed. Before she could react, it rushed toward her again.

Diana leapt off the bed. *The door!* It was unobstructed now. Her heart beat against her rib cage. She needed to outrun this thing—she needed to reach the Amazons.

But before she could get to the door's brass handle, it lunged across the floor. Diana gasped as it grabbed her by the ankle. She fell face forward, her head hitting the marble floor.

"Let me go!" she shouted, kicking.

Firmly gripping an ankle, the figure dragged her backward, away from the door and toward the window. *What's it doing?* Diana wondered. They were fifty feet above the ground! Was it going to throw her out the window?

Diana grasped at the floor, but the marble was too smooth for her to grip. Her sword was too far away. The being continued methodically dragging her toward the window, its hold frighteningly tight.

But then—a book! A thick tome on local history was splayed near her. If she threw it at the figure, maybe she could distract it. It was worth a try. Straining, she inched her fingers toward the book. Her cheeks flushed from the effort. Her arms ached, but then—she had it! Drawing it to her, she glowered with all her might, then hurled it at the creature.

Instantly, the figure shot a hand shot up as a whirring sound bellowed from deep within its cloaked body. Before Diana could react, a burst of metallic-gold powder sprang from one of its sleeves. The powder coated the book, which froze in midair and then burst into flames. Within seconds it fell to the floor, transformed into ashes.

A chill passed through Diana. *What is this thing?*

It grasped at the glass now and fumbled against the latch. Diana had only seconds until it opened the window and did whatever it was planning to do to her. She glanced around frantically at the floor—there had to be some way to stop it. Suddenly her eyes brightened. A belt. A shiny silver one had fallen to the ground. It was inches away.

The window latch clicked open.

Diana edged her hand toward the belt. Drawing her fingers around it, she grasped it and yanked it toward her.

The window parted a crack.

Looping the belt, she hurriedly fashioned it into

a lasso. It wasn't the Lasso of Truth—but it would have to do.

"And now," she muttered under her breath, "I get you."

Channeling every ounce of strength she had, Diana slammed her one free leg hard against the creature's back. Its grip loosened for a fraction of a second. Diana wrestled free, leapt up, and swung the loop around its body.

The being tugged at the makeshift lasso in a panic, but Diana's grip was firm. Again the whirring sound trumpeted from within. Golden powder burst from its sleeves, but with its arms trapped tight against its body, to Diana's relief it only managed to scorch the marble floor beneath it.

"Time for some answers," Diana said in a low voice.

Suddenly, the creature screeched. Diana shuddered at the high-pitched, terrifying sound.

"Make all the noises you want," she said, as it struggled against her grip. "You're not going anywhere now."

She tugged on the belt, drawing the figure toward her.

"Now let's see who you are." Diana reached to grab its hood, but before she could push it back, the whirring sound buzzed once more and then—an explosion.

Diana flew back. Her head hit the wall. Stars danced in her vision. The burning cloak went limp against her makeshift lasso and fluttered toward the ground, disintegrating into a pile of debris.

The creature was gone.

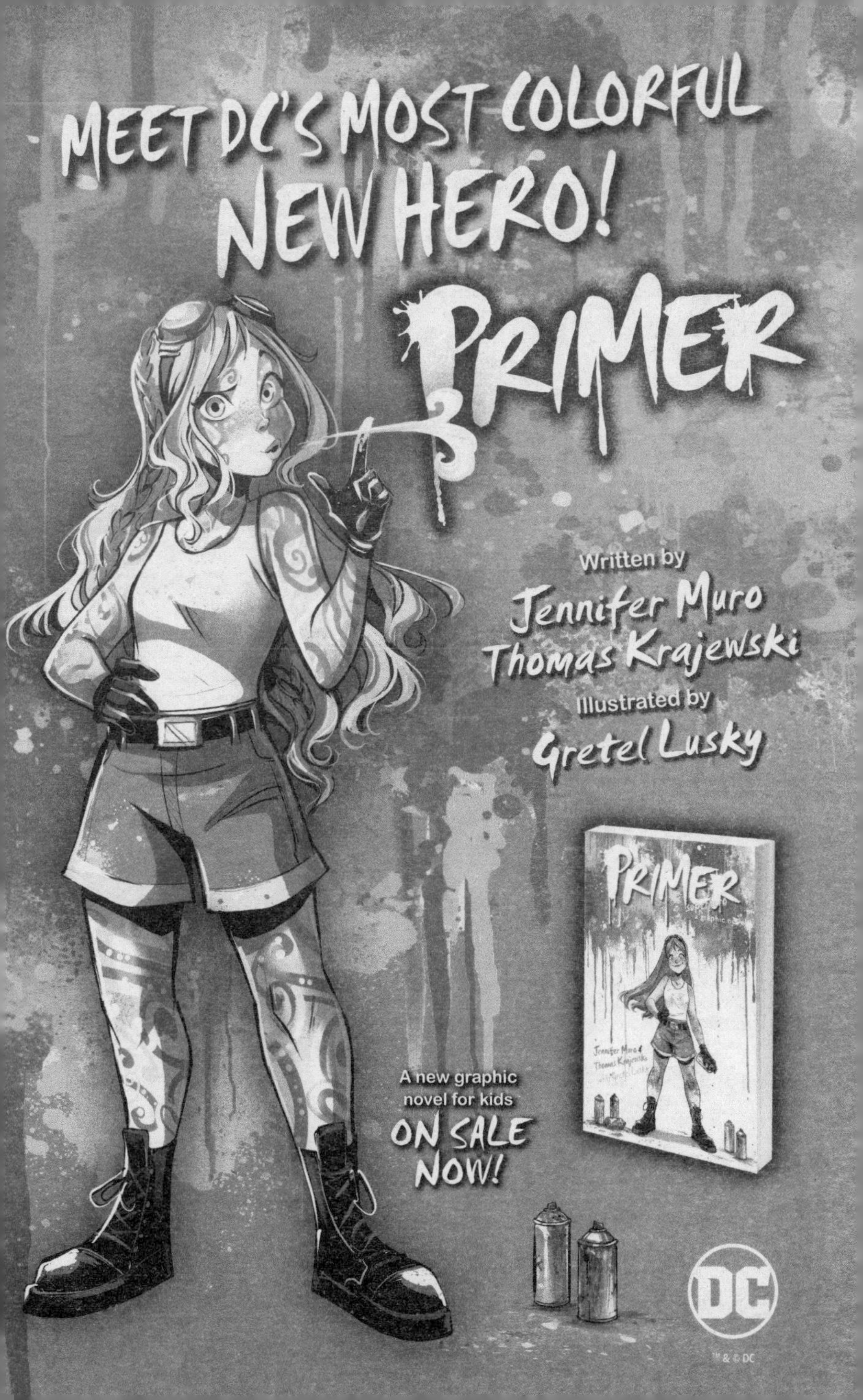
MEET DC'S MOST COLORFUL
NEW HERO!
PRIMER
Written by
Jennifer Muro
Thomas Krajewski
Illustrated by
Gretel Lusky
PRIMER
A new graphic novel for kids
ON SALE NOW!
DC
TM & © DC